Model Cars & Road Vehicles

Model Cars & Road Vehicles

Patrick Trench

Pelham Books

First published in Great Britain by
Pelham Books Ltd
44 Bedford Square
London WC1B 3DU
1983

British Library Cataloguing in Publication Data
Trench, Patrick
Model cars and road vehicles.
1. Automobiles – Models
I. Title
629. 2'2122 TL237

ISBN 0 7207 1468 0

Edited by Gill Freeman, Prospect Publishing

Designed by Tim McPhee and Jim Reader

Designed and produced by Book Production Consultants
47 Norfolk Street, Cambridge CB1 2LE
for
Prospect Publishing Co Ltd
24 Arlington Gardens
Chiswick, London W4 4EY

Printed in Hong Kong

Half title illustration

HORNBY SERIES MODELLED MINIATURES NO 22 MOTOR VEHICLES 1933–35 E CONTAINING:**
Top Row 22A SPORTS CAR 1933–35 E* ● 22B SPORTS COUPE 1933–35 E*
2nd Row 22C MOTOR TRUCK 1933–35 E ● 22D DELIVERY VAN 1933–35 E
3rd Row 22E FARM TRACTOR 1933–41 D ● 22F ARMY TANK 1933–39 D
CALLED 'DINKY TOYS' FROM 1934

Contents

Switching on
An historical introduction

In the beginning
Although it was an Englishman, William Britain, who pioneered the hollow-cast method of lead figure manufacture, in the field of model cars England has provided very little that is innovative in terms of production methods. Yet it boasts the two most famous names, Dinky Toys and Matchbox, who in their heyday, the 1950's and 1960's respectively, achieved a virtual monopoly of the world markets in their respective sizes by providing a wide choice of models of consistently high quality.

The history of die-cast model cars, however, begins abroad. The first die-cast miniature cars, which were non-prototypical in that they were generic types of vehicle rather than models of any recognisable make, were produced by SR in France and Tootsietoy in the USA from around 1910. Although only 2 inches (50mm) long, they were finely detailed and ran on delicate, spoked wheels. They were made of a soft lead alloy, which was to remain the principal material for die-cast toy cars until the early 1930's.

The first recognisable prototype to appear in miniature was the famous Model 'T' Ford, different versions of which were produced by both these companies from around 1915. The pick up version of the Tootsietoy was later copied by Johillco in England. The length was increased to 3 inches (76mm) giving the models a scale of approximately $^1/_{48}$th which set the precedent for the majority of models until the Second World War.

By the late 1920's Tootsietoy had established itself as the world's most prolific and innovative manufacturer of die-cast toys. Among its achievements was the first model car to have a separately-cast radiator grille: the Ford Model 'A', issued in 1928. Tootsietoy's success in this period can be seen by the number of copies which were made of their products, both in the USA and in Europe, particularly by Johillco in England (despite the fact that the vehicles represented are typically American), and by the use of their assembly methods by every major pre-war manufacturer.

Their two most important contributions are contained in a series of models of Graham cars, issued in 1933. Firstly they developed a common chassis with a variety of different body styles, the two parts being held together by the axles. The 'three-part construction' (the third part being the separate radiator grille, now plated for greater realism) was adopted by all the major European manufacturers in the following years, for example by Märklin in Germany, SR in France and Dinky Toys in England. Their second innovation, and the one that is more important to model car manufacture, was the change of material from lead, to a zinc alloy called zamak or mazak (the other letters in the name refer to magnesium, aluminium and copper, the other constituents of the alloy). This alloy has the advantage of being both lighter and stronger, so that finer and more accurate castings could be made with no reduction in rigidity. Unfortunately, it has the disadvantage that even very low levels of impurity in the alloy can lead to the metal becoming brittle and gradually disintegrating with time, a phenomenom known to collectors as 'fatigue'. (See page 92.)

As a final word on Tootsietoy's contribution to model car manufacture, it is worth mentioning that from the mid 1920's the vast majority of their castings had recessed rather than raised lines around the doors and bonnet – a feature which did not become standard in European toy cars until the late 1950's

British die-casts
The first British die-cast vehicles were produced very much as a side-line by manufacturers of civilian and military lead figures. It is difficult to determine who came first, but by about 1930 small ranges of vehicles were being produced by Johillco, Charbens, and Taylor and Barrett. Most of Johillco's (John Hill Co) and Charbens' (Charles Benson) models in these early years were copies of Tootsietoys, so the distinction of having produced the first totally original toy road vehicles in this country probably goes to Taylor and Barrett (T & B). Of two-, later three-part construction, though of a different pattern to that used by Tootsietoy, they were generic types of vehicle rather than models of particular makes, and are both crude and charming.

Johillco's first original efforts were three hollow-cast lead record cars produced in the early 1930's. In the following years the firm produced a small number of other vehicles, both original and copied, but it remained primarily a figures manufacturer.

Charbens likewise produced few original models, but

was responsible for the majority of the relatively few English examples of slush-casting. In this process, which was extensively used by the cheaper American manufacturers, the molten lead is poured into a hollow mould, spun out by hand to fill the extremities, then poured out leaving a layer of variable thickness. Only the exterior is formed, the inside having a rough finish. The process is similar to that used for making hollow-cast figures.

Britains, the largest of the figure manufacturers, produced very few cars or other road vehicles in comparison with their ranges of farm and military vehicles, and the majority were to the larger scale of $^1/_{32}$nd, the standard scale for their figures. The exceptions were two finely-cast record cars issued in the mid- and late 1930's.

Enter Dinky

Until the first Dinky Toys appeared, England was providing very little which could compete with the imported Tootsietoys. Dinky's first offering, the 22 Motor Vehicles set, comprising two cars, two lorries, a tractor and a tank, appeared in late 1933 under the the title 'Hornby Series Modelled Miniatures'. The series had begun in 1931 with the appearance of some sets of lead figures for stations, and the vehicles were similarly intended to add detail to '0' gauge railway layouts, although being to a scale of about $^1/_{48}$th they were in fact slightly too small. They were cast in lead alloy, and the road vehicles ran on solid metal wheels. Their immediate and enormous success was not due to their quality, for they were neither better nor worse than the Tootsietoys of the period, but rather because they were produced by the makers of the already famous Meccano and

Hornby Trains, and were the first home-produced toy cars to be adequately marketed and distributed. To help in this latter respect, the name was changed to 'Meccano Miniatures' in early 1934, and then to 'Meccano Dinky Toys' in April of that year.

At the same time, three new sets were announced which were more typical of pre-war Dinky Toys production – a set of eight cars (series 24), a set of six lorries (series 25), and a set of six delivery vans with advertising (series 28). Many of the pre-war Dinky Toys were retailed both in boxed sets of six or eight, and individually without boxes, although the individual items were supplied to the retailer in boxes of six. The classification of a series number denoting the type of vehicle, followed by a letter for each model within the series, such as 24b Limousine, 25d Petrol Tanker, remained until the mid-1950's, when it was replaced by an all-number system which retained the number as an indication of the type of vehicle.

While the vans were made of lead, using the casting from one of the original series 22 (later replaced by a one-piece mazak casting), the cars and lorries were more up-to-date and featured all the improvements pioneered by Tootsietoy in the previous year.

They were made of mazak, as were almost all subsequent Dinkies, were of an identical three-part construction pattern to that employed by the American firm, and ran on metal hubs fitted with detachable rubber tyres. These three sets, with some minor casting changes (and a major one in the case of the vans, as mentioned above) continued in production until the

DINKY TOY 36G TAXI WITH DRIVER
YELLOW/BLACK AND RED/BLACK 1938–41 B ● GREEN/BLACK AND MAROON/BLACK 1946–48 B

war, and the lorries, with further minor changes, continued until about 1950.

As casting techniques improved, one-piece castings were more widely used, especially as this method was better for reflecting the smoother lines of real vehicles. A further advantage was that since there was no need to make the body fit a standardised chassis, the proportions of the real vehicle could be more accurately followed. The next refinement was the insertion of a tin-plate baseplate, a practice started by Märklin of Germany in about 1934 and first used on some very Märklin-like Dinky Toys issued in 1936. Up till 1939, the baseplates were largely decorative, since the axles were still held through holes in the body casting. In that year, however, two new sets were announced (though they may not have been issued until 1940) which set standards for casting detail and construction method which were not substantially improved until the very late 1950's. Each of the cars – six sports cars (series 38), only three of which actually appeared before production ceased in 1941, and six American cars (series 39), had the name of the car stamped on the baseplate. More significant still, the baseplates of the sports cars and of the Lincoln from the 39 series were functional: they were rivetted to the body casting and held the axles in place. The sports cars had transparent celluloid windscreens – the first example of plastic windows on die-cast cars – which were also held in place by the baseplate.

A final point on pre-war Dinky Toys: although none issued before 1939 were identified on the toy (some of the models with tinplate baseplates were later altered to include the name) and only a dozen or so were identified in Meccano literature, most of them were models of real vehicles, although the degree of accuracy varied considerably.

Post-war developments

The immediate post-war period witnessed the emergence of a great many small die-cast toy manufacturers, for a variety of reasons. The war had trained a large number of mould makers (of varying levels of skill, it should be added), and the public had been so starved of toys it would buy almost *anything* with four wheels. As with all 'booms', the number of failures outweighed the successes. Only a handful of manufacturers survived more than a few years. The rest sank into obscurity.

The rapid rise and fall of these companies was partly a reflection of the business strength of Dinky Toys. The firm lost little time in recommencing production. The toys were seen as a very saleable commodity in those export markets which Britain badly needed, having incurred a massive war debt. Only small quantities appeared in toyshops at home. The bulk of the production comprised re-issues of pre-war items and, as far as exports were concerned, it was fortunate that these included the 39 series of American cars since America was the prime market and Tootsietoy's standards had dropped drastically owing to increased labour charges.

Although few new releases appeared in the period up till 1952, some of them were significant. A new range of lorries which appeared in late 1947, called 'Dinky Super-toys' was the first British example of die-cast lorries to be made to the same scale as the cars, though this had been achieved by Märklin before the war. Previously toys had all been made to the same size, so lorries were to a considerably smaller scale. Once Dinkies started to re-appear in quantity, of course, there was little room left for four-wheeled 'blobs'.

Before the new names are introduced, here is a resume of the post-war histories of the manufacturers from the pre-war era. Johillco, although it continued to produce figures for some years, appears to have made no road vehicles after the war. T & B had by now split up into Barrett and Sons (B & S), who re-issued a trolley-bus from one of the old moulds, and F G Taylor (F G T), who produced three simplified versions of T & B vehicles, a coach, a fire engine and racing car, in the late 1940's. Although these two firms continued to make lead, later plastic, figures and accessories until very recently, including many from pre-war moulds, they made no further vehicles. Charbens continued to make road vehicles along with the figures until the company's demise in the early 1960's. The material had changed to mazak and the casting were generally rather crude. They also made a small series of hollow-cast racing cars in the mid-1950's. The extreme rarity of these models today shows that the experiment failed!

The new names in die-cast cars to emerge in the period from 1946 to 1953 can be categorised according to what might be called 'original function', or what the company

NON-DINKY VEHICLES OF THE 1930'S

Top Row TAYLOR AND BARRETT FIRE ENGINE AND WHEELED ESCAPE D ● TAYLOR AND BARRETT BREAKDOWN TRUCK C
2nd Row TAYLOR AND BARRETT STREAMLINE COACH D ● TAYLOR AND BARRETT PETROL TANKER C ● TAYLOR AND BARRETT TROLLEY-BUS C (post-war example (B & S); pre-war issue says 'Champion Malt Vinegar')
3rd Row TAYLOR AND BARRETT AMBULANCE C ● TAYLOR AND BARRETT STREAMLINE SALOON C ● TAYLOR AND BARRETT SALOON CAR C (broken rear wings and replaced radiator grille)
4th Row DYSON SS1 COUPE C (repainted) ● JOHILLCO 630L FORD MODEL 'T' PICK-UP B (repainted) ● CHARBENS AMBULANCE C (repainted)
5th Row BRITAINS 1400 MALCOLM CAMPBELL'S BLUEBIRD III 1935–40 E

was producing before turning to die-casting. These categories are by no means arbitrary as the 'original function' is reflected in the maker's approach. The three categories are: figures manufacturers; tinplate manufacturers; and firms with little or no previous experience in toy-making.

As in pre-war days, the figures manufacturers' view was that just as the lead soldier is not a model of a particular person, the toy car need not be an accurate model of a real car. The vehicles were seen as accessories to the figures rather than the other way around. This approach can be seen in the early post-war Charbens vehicles, and in those of two of the new names, Crescent and Timpo, both of whom had been making figures since before the war. Their early vehicles were one-piece mazak castings and were crude in appearance. Yet in this period when few good cheap models were available, they were very popular. Timpo, who had the larger range, turned to plastic vehicles in the early 1950's, but figures remained its primary product. Crescent produced the classic cheap toy car of the period: bearing a passing resemblance to a Jaguar saloon, it sits on four thin metal wheels, often badly cast so that they cannot turn. Large numbers have survived as evidence of its popularity. The company went on to make a series of excellent racing car models in the mid-1950's, but by this time Dinky Toys had re-established their monopoly and Crescent made few further attempts at road vehicles. The company was sold to Lone Star in 1981.

The tinplate manufacturers' approach was that a toy is a toy, even if it is a model, so most of their die-cast products were fitted with clock-work or inertia (friction) motors. Wells-Brimtoy, Chad Valley and Mettoy were three of the largest tinplate toy producers in the country both before and after the war. Wells-Brimtoy's die-cast range, called 'Pocketoys' was limited to five models in all, but three of them are significant in that they represent British cars of a period not touched by Dinky Toys. The firm continued to produce tinplate and plastic toys, and is still in existence. Chad Valley's first die-casts were some generic cars and lorries issued in the late 1940's. At the same time, they were commissioned by the Rootes Group, the makers of Hillman, Humber, Sunbeam and Commer, to make some promotional models.

The results were some fair, some excellent clockwork models of Rootes Group vehicles, which were sold both in Rootes garages and in toy shops. The firm made some further die-cast vehicles in various sizes until the mid-1950's, but most of these fall outside the scope of this book. Mettoy later changed the face of British die-casts with the Corgi Toys range; already at the time of its first attempts at die-cast toys, in the late 1940's, the products were well made. The firm was evidently experimenting with the market: rather than produce a range of vehicles to one size and in one material, it made the same two cars in four different sizes from 2 inches (50mm) to 12 inches (300mm) the largest being in plastic, the smaller ones being available in plastic or metal, with friction or clock-work motors. Judging by their subsequent activities, one presumes that the best sellers were the 4 inch (100mm) examples in metal!

The third category, the new firms, were in the long term the most successful to emerge from this period. Lesney, Benbros and Morestone all commenced production from small factories in the North-East of London, a very fertile area as far as toy manufacture is

PRE-WAR DINKY TOY ACCESSORIES

45 GARAGE 1935–40 C CONTAINING:
24C TOWN SEDAN 1934–40 E ● 42C POINT DUTY POLICEMAN WHITE COAT 1936–41 A ●
42D POINT DUTY POLICEMAN 1936–41 A ● 43A RAC BOX 1935–40 B

concerned, having already provided such names as Britains, Charbens, Crescent, Wells and Brimtoy.

The firm of Lesney, the name being a combination of the names of two of the three founders, Leslie and Rodney, was formed in 1947 to manufacture commercial die-casting for other companies, an activity it continued to pursue until very recently. Among these products were toys. They must have had a particular appeal for in 1949 Lesney began to make its own toys as a side-line to its commercial casting work. The firm's early range of horse-drawn and motor vehicles included some of the largest die-cast models made at the time, in striking contrast to the range which was to make it famous. The quality of the castings was at least as good as that of the Dinky Toys of the period, but sales potential was no doubt hampered by the lack of consistency in terms of either scale or size. The last remark applies to the early products of both Benbros (Benenson Brothers) who, after a brief and unsuccessful attempt at lead figure manufacture, started to produce die-cast toys in about 1950, and Morestone (Morris and Stone) who, combined with the die-casting firm of Modern Products Ltd, set up operations at about the same time. The geographical proximity of the three companies and the fact that they were all relative new-comers led, intentionally or not, to a certain amount of exchange of ideas. As a result some of their early efforts are very similar. In addition, similar toys were being produced for Moko (Moses Kohnstam), the company later responsible for marketing Lesney's products. Further confusion is caused by the fact that Lesney was still making toys for other companies and that most of these toys are either marked simply 'Made in England' or not at all. The original boxes, where they exist, are sometimes more helpful in aiding identification.

The impact of Lesney

The turning point for Lesney came in 1953, when it re-issued a large model of the State Processional Coach, originally made in 1950, to celebrate the coronation of Queen Elizabeth II. At the same time, the company released a scaled-down version of the same coach which, despite being only 4½ inches (114mm) long, lacked little of the detail of the larger one. The small version was immensely popular, over a million examples were sold in

1953, demonstrating the potential demand for smaller toys. As a result, the first three Matchbox Series models were released in the same year and met with immediate success.

Within the next two years both Benbros and Morestone had followed with their own series of miniatures, and even copied the idea of the novelty-style box. Benbros's TV Series models came in boxes resembling television sets. The series was later re-titled 'Mighty Midgets' and these came in normal boxes – while Morestone's miniatures were sold in boxes resembling Esso petrol pumps. By this time, however, Lesney was issuing new Matchbox models at the rate of 12 a year and although the small Morestones were often of similar quality, Lesney's superior marketing and distribution were already making Matchbox a household name.

By 1960, the year in which the first Matchbox 75 appeared (since when there have always been 75 models in the Matchbox series), Lesney had established itself as the market leader in its size range, both at home and in America, a position which was not seriously threatened for almost ten years. Benbros and Morestone continued to produce small models until about 1961 and 1967 respectively, the latter company having changed its name to 'Budgie Toys' in 1960. Neither of them was to make any Matchbox-sized toys with such features as windows or opening parts, which started to appear on Matchbox models from 1960.

Before describing the other ranges produced by these companies, a few points on the subject of small-scale models. Firstly, although it was undoubtedly the most successful, Lesney was by no means the first company to attempt to cast such small models. The little SR's mentioned at the beginning of this introduction, which are probably the oldest cast toy cars ever made, are in very much the same size range as the first Matchboxes, and smaller ranges of similarly-sized toys were produced by Britains and Johillco in lead and by Dinky Toys in mazak before the war. The nearest equivalents to Matchbox being produced at the time were probably a series by Mercury of Italy from the late 1940's, and the small plastic Wiking Models from Germany, but neither of these ranges was widely exported. Secondly, the interest in smaller-scaled models at the time when the Matchbox Series first appeared was no doubt due to the almost

LESSER-KNOWN MANUFACTURERS OF THE 1950'S

Top Row MORESTONE/BUDGIE 5 WOLSELEY 6/80 POLICE CAR 1955–67 A ● BUDGIE 27 WOLSELEY 6/80 FIRE CAR early 1960'S A ● BUDGIE 5 WOLSELEY 6/80 SQUAD CAR mid-1960'S A ● BUDGIE 272 GERRY ANDERSON'S 'SUPERCAR' *ca* 1962–67 C

2nd Row DCMT RIVER SERIES STANDARD VANGUARD PHASE II mid-1950'S B ● METTOY 602 STANDARD VANGUARD *ca* 1949–55 B ● DCMT LONE STAR ROADMASTERS DAIMLER CONQUEST ROADSTER late 1950'S B

3rd Row MORESTONE/MODERN PRODUCT DAIMLER AMBULANCE 1950'S B (as Budgie 258 with ambulance transfers and red chassis, early 1960'S B) ● MORESTONE/ MODERN PRODUCT WOLSELEY 6/80 POLICE CAR 1950'S B (as Budgie 246 with police signs on grille and boot, early 1960'S B) ● CHAD VALLEY 9504 GUY VAN 'LYONS' early 1950'S D

4th Row BRIMTOY-POCKETOY SUNBEAM-TALBOT 2-LITRE late 1940'S B ● BRIMTOY-POCKETOY VAUXHALL 10 COUPE late 1940'S B (repainted) ● BRIMTOY-POCKETOY VAUXHALL 14 SALOON late 1940'S B

5th Row CHAD VALLEY 9238 SUNBEAM-TALBOT 80/90 early 1950'S D ● CHAD VALLEY 9237 HUMBER SUPER SNIPE early 1950'S D ● CHAD VALLEY 9507 HUMBER HAWK early 1950'S D

universal replacement of '0' gauge by '00' gauge electric railways. A mere handful of the Dinky Toys in production at the time could be used with this gauge. A late and rather unsuccessful attempt was made with a series called 'Dublo Dinky Toys' in the late 1950's and early 1960's, which was no doubt a response to the serious effect Matchbox toys were beginning to have on Dinky's sales.

While their small products were made to a standard size, the larger Benbros and Morestone products continued to have no conformity of either size or scale. The last Benbros series, called 'Zebra Toys' and started in the early 1960's, displays the widest range of sizes. Though the standards of casting and finish were generally a great improvement on previous efforts, some of the models having more up-to-date features such as windows and plastic interior detail, they were clearly not a success, for the firm was bought out in 1965, having released only a dozen or so examples. With the change of name to 'Budgie Toys', Morestone embarked on a more successful range which grew to 60 different models by the mid-1960's. Though the quality was rarely to the standard of Dinky or Corgi, the choice of subject was often interesting. A drastically reduced range of 'Budgie Models' as they are now called, is being produced exclusively for London souvenir shops, including a Routemaster bus which has been in continuous production for over 20 years! Finally, to Morestone goes the credit of having made the first die-cast character vehicles in this country, Noddy and His Car in two sizes in the late 1950's, and Gerry Anderson's Supercar in the early 1960's.

1956 saw the launch of Lesney's famous 'Models of Yesteryear' series, a response to the public's fast-growing interest in veteran and vintage transport and almost certainly the world's first die-cast models of non-contemporaneous subjects. From the outset, there were two factors which ensured the success of the series and have maintained its position as the biggest seller in its field. The first was that the models were no more expensive than other toys of their size, so they could be afforded by children. The second was that despite this the models were sufficiently detailed and accurate to appeal to adult enthusiasts of the real vehicles for display as ornaments. In this way, they created a new market –

toys for adult collectors – though the company continues to stress that this accounts for a very small proportion of the toy market as a whole.

In the early years, Benbros and Charbens attempted to emulate the success of the Yesteryears with smaller models of veteran cars, Benbros as part of its 'Mighty Midgets' series, Charbens with a series called 'Old Crocks', that popular nick-name of the day for veteran cars.

Lesney's other products, curiously, have never been as successful as their competitors. The 'Major Pack' series, launched in the same year as the Models of Yesteryear, comprised models of large vehicles to roughly the same scale as the smaller vehicles in the Matchbox series. These were superceded in the early 1960's by the larger 'King Size' series, a rather belated first attempt to enter the Dinky-size market, which had already been joined by Corgi Toys and Spot-On. Again, these were mostly models of commercial vehicles and earth-moving equipment, but cars started to be included from the late 1960's.

The last company to be mentioned whose origins date back to the period 1946–53, again based in North London, is DCMT (Die-Cast Metal Toys). As with Lesney, the firm's first toys were for other companies, for example some of the early post-war Crescent die-casts are marked 'DCMT Crescent'. As with so many of the manufacturers already mentioned from this period, the full story of who made what for whom is yet to be determined, and many of DCMT's early products are again not marked with the manufacturer's name. Probably the first vehicles which can be attributed to them are the 'River Series', which comprised some ugly non-prototypical lorries and some reasonable models of saloon cars from the 1952–54 period. The next series, called 'Road-Masters' and comprising a small number of contemporary open cars as well as some poor models of veteran cars, was the first to bear the company's new trade name 'Lone Star'. Some $1/50$ scale American cars followed in 1960. Ironically, these rather mediocre models were marketed in the USA by Tootsietoy, once the masters in die-cast toy cars, in an attempt to revive interest in the old name. The range was abandoned after a few years in favour of the 'Impy' series of Matchbox-sized vehicles.

Corgi takes on the competition

None of the manufacturers mentioned above really offered what could be called serious competition to Dinky Toys on its own terms. The phenomenal success of 'Matchbox' obviously had an affect on sales, but was unlikely to dissuade the Dinky devotee, since the toys were incompatible. A certain level of complacency had set in at the Dinky Toys factory. Although production standards remained high, only a third of the models in production at the beginning of 1956 were of vehicles that had been introduced in the previous five years, a handful of the rest were actually of pre-war origin with no new features. Thus, when Mettoy-Playcraft introduced the all-new Corgi Toys range later that year, the Meccano factory was ill-prepared for direct competition.

The Corgi attack was extremely well planned, as you would expect from a company whose roots went back to the great days of German tin-plate toys. Not only were all the models of new vehicles, the quality of casting and the scale being compatible with Dinky Toys, but from the start the company also adopted a policy of continuous innovation, which contrasted strongly with Dinky's more conservative approach.

Three innovations appeared on the first Corgi Toys, all of which were to be adopted by Dinky within the next three years. Two of them, shiny aluminium hubs and treaded tyres, were relatively minor, yet they added to the realism of the models. The third innovation, the one used by Corgi as its advertising slogan, was a one-piece clear plastic insert for the windows, which became increasingly important in the following years as more and more cars featured 'wrapround' windows. Where space permitted, the early Corgis were available with or without friction motors, a legacy of their Mettoy parentage, but the motors used were unreliable, and the idea was abandoned in 1959. The mechanised version had cast, rather than tin-plate baseplates, and this became a standard feature of Corgi Toys from 1959. This helped to make the toys more robust, particularly when opening parts appeared which weakened the body casting.

It took Dinky Toys two years to reply by fitting windows to its own models, and from that time a contest developed. Both companies introduced spring suspension in 1959, Corgi's models also having vacuum-formed plastic interior detail. Dinky followed suit in 1960, and countered with a rather basic form of steering. In the same year, Corgi issued the first British die-cast with opening bonnet and detailed engine (the Aston Martin DB4), while the first jewelled lights appeared on Corgi's Bentley Continental the following year. The Dinky Toy MGB, issued in 1962, was the first to have opening doors, while in 1963, Corgi produced a model of the Ghia L64 with opening boot, bonnet and doors, tilting front seats and plated plastic bumpers front and rear. The suspension was now part of the hard plastic interior and this, coupled with plastic bumpers, meant that the models were becoming less durable.

In general, the fit of the opening parts was far superior on Corgi models, and the castings were cleaner and more accurate, so that from the early 1960's Dinky's share of the market began to decline, never to regain the prestige that it had enjoyed for over twenty years.

Corgi made a less successful attempt to break the Matchbox market with the 'Husky' range, launched in the early 1960's and becoming 'Corgi Juniors' in 1970.

The high point of Corgi's early career, in terms of technique if not commercial success, came in 1964 with the introduction of the first models in the 'Corgi Classics' range. These remain without doubt the finest models of veteran and vintage cars ever made by a toy manufacturer. Unfortunately, the level of detail meant that they cost almost three times as much as contemporary Models of Yesteryear, and only five basic models appeared before the series was dropped in 1969. Dinky Toys attempted to follow suit with two veteran models issued in 1964 and 1965, which despite being considerably more expensive had little to offer over Yesteryears and lasted a mere four years.

Spot-On

Another range which included vintage models at this time was Spot-On, which was the most recently-launched range of die-cast vehicles and ultimately the shortest-lived, spanning as it did nine years' production. Spot-Ons were produced by Tri-Ang at their Belfast factory from 1959. This was a surprisingly late entry into the die-cast market by one of the oldest and most prolific of British toy manufacturers. Founded in 1919 by the three Lines Brothers (the partnership of three giving rise to the triangular trade mark and the 'Tri-Ang' name) the company's products included wooden and stuffed toys, dolls, dolls' houses and prams, pedal cars and children's cycles, sheet-steel and tin-plate toys, including the famous 'Minic' range of small clockwork tin-plate vehicles which was launched at about the same time as Dinky Toys. It was probably the first toy manufacturer in this country to use plastics extensively (bakelite apart). Even before the war plastic parts were being used on some of the Minic range. In the 1950's, the company also produced '00' gauge electric railways, and later bought out the manufacturers of the 'Scalextric' slot car-racing system. When Meccano Ltd was acquired in 1964, the Spot-On range was abandoned in favour of the Dinky (the moulds for Spot-Ons were transferred to New Zealand), before the Lines Brothers group went into liquidation itself in 1971.

From the start, Spot On models had windows and interiors like their competitors' – these features were also included in the commercial vehicles, which was not standard procedure with Dinky or Corgi until the early 1960's. Later suspension and plastic bumpers were also introduced. Relatively few Spot-Ons had opening parts. Detail and finish was seldom as good as on contemporary Corgi Toys, though good choice of subject compensated for this. However, it is the aspect of scale which makes the range important.

A question of scale

As mentioned before, most pre-war Dinky Toy cars and vans were made to scales of around $1/48$th full size (the actual range being 1:45 to 1:55), while larger vehicles were made to scales of between 1:60 and 1:90. After the war the scales increased slightly – European cars and vans were to scales of between 1:45 and 1:48, and American cars between 1:48 and 1:50. The scales of commercial vehicles continued to vary widely, though the Supertoys models fell into the same 1:45 to 1:50 bracket as the cars. The tendency was for smaller vehicles to be a larger scale than larger vehicles, so that the relative sizes of the real vehicles was lost in the toys. The scales of Corgi Toys were very much the same as those of comparable Dinky Toys. By the late 1950's however, there was a growing tendency among European manufacturers to standardise the scales of their models. Interestingly it was the French Dinky Toy factory which started this trend. Every French Dinky European car introduced after the war was made to a scale of 1:43, the actual scale of '0' gauge railways, but for some reason the English factory did not follow this lead. American cars produced at the French factory, were made to $1/48$th scale, this scale being more popular in America as it corresponded to their 'S' gauge railways. French Dinky commercials, on the other hand, continued to be to considerably smaller scales. By 1960, a two-tier scale system had developed, adopted by Dinky Toys (France) and several other manufacturers, notably Solido (France) and Tekno (Denmark), whereby cars and light commercials were made to $1/43$rd scale, and larger commercials to $1/50$th scale.

Spot-On was unique in that *every* model in the range, from micro-car to double-decker bus, was made to a constant $1/42$nd scale, this being easier to calculate than

DINKY TOY AMBULANCES

24A CREAM AND RED 1934–41 D ● 30F GREY AND RED 1935–38 C (reproduction radiator grille).
The chassis was replaced by one with full front wings in 1938, issued in the same colours to 1941.
The three with black chassis are 30F 1946–48 C (open windows on early post-war issue; grey is scarcer colour)

$1/43$rd. This feature extended to all the accessories in the range as well. Tri-Ang had in fact claimed that its Minic range was 'all to the same scale' back in the 1930's, but this was not entirely true. Dinky scales started to increase as a result, and from the time of the Lines Brothers take-over in 1964, the majority of Dinky Toys were made to $1/42$nd scale. The scale of Corgi Toys also increased slightly, but remained inconsistent, most vehicles being in the 1:42 to 1:45 range until the mid-1970's. The size of Matchbox vehicles grew from around $2\frac{1}{2}$ inches (60mm) to 3 inches (75mm) during the 1960's, but for a different reason: the larger size made it possible to include more features such as opening parts.

In the late 1960's, Matchbox's sales in America were severely hit by the appearance of a new range of small cars called 'Hot Wheels', which had thin axles and low-friction wheel bearings. The complacency which affected the company at the time, much the same as that encountered in Dinky Toys up to 1956, was quickly overcome, and in 1970 the majority of the vehicles were converted to 'Superfast' wheels. Low-friction wheels had already begun to appear on Dinky (Speed-wheels) and Corgi (Whizzwheels) cars in the previous year, and were later introduced on Corgi Juniors and Lone Star Flyers, most of which were converted 'Impy' vehicles.

Another change of scale started to take place from around 1972, when the first models in a new series of Corgi $1/36$th scale racing cars appeared. Within a few years, saloon cars were also produced to this scale and since 1977 Corgi has been, finally, the most consistent British manufacturer in this respect. Some of the last Dinky Toys to be made before the Liverpool factory closed in November 1979 were to $1/35$th scale, while an increasing number of Matchbox 'Superkings' (the name given to 'King Size' models when fitted with fast wheels) and Models of Yesteryear are being made to similar scales.

Marketing

As with any competitive industry, the promotion of the toys has an impact on sales, though it was never taken as seriously as, for example, by the manufacturers of full-size vehicles. Of the major companies, only Corgi attempted a street hoarding campaign, for a brief period in 1981, and advertisements for toy cars rarely featured outside toy trade journals. New Dinky Toys were featured in the *Meccano Magazine*, and in the mid-1960's announcements of new Dinky and Corgi models appeared in boys' comics. The full range of Dinky Toys was shown only in general 'Meccano Products' catalogues until 1953, when the first fully-illustrated Dinky Toys catalogue was printed. Similar catalogues were issued every year thereafter until 1978. The first Corgi and Matchbox catalogues were issued in 1957, and for the first few years a sheet illustrating some of the range was included in each Corgi box. To promote customer loyalties, Dinky, Corgi and Spot-On each had a collectors' club for a few years, which offered little beyond a badge, a membership certificate and advance announcements of new releases. These clubs were moderately successful, but the amount of administration involved finally outweighed the benefit to the company.

All Dinky Toys vehicles had individual boxes from 1954, where previously these had been reserved for the larger models only, and the other major manufacturers' products were packaged in this way. Until the mid-1960's, the box was made of card, the thickness of which depended on the weight of the contents, usually with an illustration of the model on one or more sides. From this time, window boxes, with two sides of the box replaced by thin transparent plastic, were used for Corgis, Spot-Ons, Lone Star and Lesney King Size and Models of Yesteryear. Blister packs, where a bubble of clear plastic containing the toy is glued to a card backing which can be hung vertically, were unsuccessfully used for the Dinky Toy racing cars in the early 1960's, but were later adopted for Corgi Juniors. Dinky Toys used some very space-consuming packaging in the early 1970's, before deciding on the by now standard window box pattern.

Collectors

There have always been a small number of adult collectors of toy cars, particularly since the introduction of the Models of Yesteryear series. In recent years the number of collectors of old toys in general, and of die-cast cars in particular, has swelled enormously. It is hard to put forward a rationale for this, in as much as it is difficult to say why people collect things at all, but it seems to be a reflection of the search for amusement in troubled times and of a feeling of nostalgia. There is also the element of investment, for the prices of some toys have risen dramatically in a very short time, though it can still remain a relatively cheap hobby. The recent boom in toy collecting has brought about a shortening of the time span between the production of the toy and its interest to collectors: ten years ago a toy car with windows would have been considered too new by most serious collectors, whereas now there is as much interest in many of the 1960's models, and even in some of those made in the 1970's, as there is in the earlier issues. Prejudices against plastic parts and low-friction wheels are being rapidly eroded. Not all today's playthings will be collectors' items tomorrow, but the British die-cast industry can still produce cars which are good toys *and* good models!

On the road
Saloon cars

The first saloon car models to be made in Britain were probably the Tootsietoy copies by Johillco. The two models chosen were a Ford Model 'A' Coupé and the Sedan, which despite being a model of a 1922 Yellow Cab, strictly speaking a taxi rather than a saloon, was never identified as such by either company. These copies appeared around 1930 and were probably made until the second World War. Despite the relatively long production runs, they are among the scarcer Johillco copies, and are much harder to find than the original Tootsies.

Rarer still are some die-cast mazak copies of Tootsietoy's famous Graham series made by an as-yet unidentified English company (probably Johillco) in the mid-1930's. On the subject of rarity, it should be noted that this does not necessarily imply a high price on the collectors' market. Despite their historical interest, these early die-casts are largely ignored by British collectors.

The Taylor and Barrett cars are again among the scarcer vehicles by this firm. The T & B Saloon Car merits particular mention since it was the *only* attempt to portray the typical British family car of the mid-1930's; a small four-door saloon with upright body-work and a small boot at the rear. Also in the range is a Streamline Saloon with the airflow style beloved of toy manufacturers at the time, if not by the car-buying public.

The first Dinky Toy saloons appeared in the 24 Series Motor Cars set, made from 1934 to 1940 or 1941. Like most early Dinkies, they were given generic names such as 'Limousine' and 'Town Sedan', rather than specific makes. However, four of the five saloons in the set were included in the 36 Series Motor Cars set issued in 1937, with individual radiator grilles replacing the common one used for the 24 Series, and with specific makers' names. Thus, the Limousine became an Armstrong-Siddeley, the Vogue Saloon a Humber, the Super Streamlined Saloon a Rover, and the Sportsman's Coupé a Bentley. The degree of accuracy of the model was governed by the relative sizes of the real cars since the same chassis was used for all the different bodies. Thus, in the case of the Humber Vogue, a small (and, incidentally, unsuccessful) 12HP saloon body had to be stretched to fit a chassis suitable for a limousine, making the Dinky Toy much more rakish and elegant than the real car!

The two series are sufficiently collectable to warrant a description of the main differences between them. As well as by the radiator grilles, the two series can be differentiated by the baseplates, the 24 Series being open underneath, with three bracing bars, while the 36 Series baseplate is solid, with rudimentary transmission detail cast in. Side-mounted spare wheels were fitted to most Vogue Saloons and Sportsman's Coupés, but never to their 36 Series counterparts. Finally, the 36 Series cars were originally fitted with lithographed tinplate people attached to slots in the baseplates – drivers and footmen in the Humber and Armstrong-Siddeley; drivers and passengers in the Bentley and Rover. This added detail led to increased prices, so the 24 Series was continued as a cheaper alternative.

The 36 Series was re-issued after the war, but without the figures. The fifth 24 Series saloon car was the Town Sedan, which has a very classy air with its exposed driver's seat and closed saloon at the rear. The side-mounted spare wheel it usually sports adds to the opulent impression. A Town Sedan in good condition is now the most desirable and valuable Dinky saloon car on the collectors' market, partly because there is no common post-war equivalent and partly because the vulnerability of its separately-cast dashboard/windscreen unit makes it difficult to find complete examples. As with all pre-war Dinkies cast in mazak, corrosion or fatigue is rampant in the two series, and the shorter production runs of the 36 Series cars with people makes them harder to find in good condition, although post-war examples are common enough.

Late in 1934, Dinky released a model of the very advanced Chrysler Airflow saloon, which must rate as the most modelled flop of all time. It had a one-piece body casting with separate front and rear bumpers, and was 4 inches (103mm) long. Its relatively short post-war run makes it harder to find than other post-war re-issues, but not as hard as the present price differential would suggest. Much scarcer is the 3½ inch (85mm) model of the same car made from 1935 to 1941 as a cheaper alternative. Also issued in 1935 were the last Dinky Toys of the three-part construction pattern. From the rather mixed 30 Series, which included the larger Airflow (and a caravan trailer in spite of the Motor Vehicles title), the three cars, a Rolls-Royce, a Daimler and a Vauxhall, again shared a common chassis, but this time the cars were more carefully chosen and the models are more accurate, the Rolls-Royce being particularly elegant. Most pre-war Vauxhalls have side-mounted spare wheels, and in this version are as scarce as any of the 24 Series cars, while the post-war re-issues of the three cars are still quite easy to find in fair condition.

The 36 Series cars with liveried chauffeurs and footmen are indicative of Dinky's choice of subject in the pre-war years. All the cars chosen were 'quality' cars – they were not models of the family's car, unless it was well-to-do, but of what the family might aspire to. Nor was the model of the little Austin Seven Ruby saloon, issued in 1936, an exception to this. It was the *smart* small car, a cut above the more basic small Ford, for example.

The last Dinky saloon cars released before the war were the important 39 Series American cars which, as previously stated, set standards for casting quality for many years. While the pre-war issues are scarce, post-war versions are not hard to find.

Most British cars from 1945 and 1946 were re-issued 1940 models. The only good die-cast models of cars from this period are the two Vauxhalls, a 10 coupé and a 14 saloon, and the Sunbeam-Talbot two-litre made by Brimtoy, Dinky not having released any new British saloons since 1936. When the next series of Dinky saloons was launched in 1947, it comprised entirely new cars. The first of these were a Riley two and a half litre and a Triumph Renown, continuing Dinky's preference for quality cars, soon to be joined by more mundane cars such as the Hillman Minx and Austin Devon. Up till the mid-1960's the range of subjects was quite comprehensive, a remark which holds true also for the other manufacturers of the period like Matchbox, Corgi and Spot-On.

There were, however, some omissions which in retrospect do seem to be very surprising. For example, while models of the Jaguar Mark X appeared in all four ranges, and in the Husky and Imp ranges as well, only Matchbox and Spot-on made die-cast models of the Morris Minor, despite the popularity of the real car. Even these models had relatively short production runs which make them harder to find than most toys of their age.

Very few American saloons were modelled until the late 1950's, when the introduction of windows made the new shapes easier to translate. Significant numbers started to appear in the Dinky, Corgi and Matchbox ranges reflecting the importance of the American market. A classic period piece is Corgi's Chevrolet Impala of 1959, the vulgarity of the enormous fins being accentuated by the bright pink paint!

Dinky's first European car was, predictably, a Volkswagen Beetle issued in 1956. It was not deleted until 1970, giving it the longest continuous production run for a Dinky saloon which rivalled that of the real car. From the late 1950's 'foreign' cars became more prominent in all ranges, reflecting Britain's diminishing share of real car markets. In this respect Dinky Toys and Spot-On were generally less comprehensive than their competitors, but for rather different reasons. There was a Dinky factory in France to cater for the European market, while Spot-Ons were not exported, so that the only cars available in these islands were modelled, including a Beetle of course! Indeed, Spot-On is the only range of British die-casts without any American vehicles whatsoever.

The late 1960's saw a widespread move away from family cars. Sports saloons had always been popular subjects with toy manufacturers. Spot-On had a penchant for these cars, the Bristol 406 being an example – incidentally the only model of a road-going Bristol – while Corgi's Bentley Continental was one of the firm's early highlights. But by 1970 the market was dominated by models of Lamborghinis and similar exotica. Undoubtedly the adoption of low-friction wheels called for models of faster cars, though Matchbox took this trend to extremes with the introduction of more and more futuristic designs with no resemblance to real cars.

The last few years has seen a reversal of this trend and the current Matchbox and Corgi ranges include a considerable number of 'normal' saloon cars from Europe, America and, of course, Japan, while the renewed importance of the home market can be seen in the care with which Corgi manages to release models of new British cars such as the Metro, Acclaim, Sierra and Maestro almost simultaneously with the full-size cars.

Top Row 24D VOGUE SALOON 1934–41 D ● 30G CARAVAN 1936–41 C

2nd Row 36C HUMBER VOGUE SALOON WITH DRIVER AND FOOTMAN 1937–41 E ● 36A ARMSTRONG-SIDDELEY LIMOUSINE WITH DRIVER AND FOOTMAN 1937–41 E

3rd Row 36D ROVER STREAMLINE SALOON WITH DRIVER AND PASSENGER 1937–41 E ● 35A SALOON CAR 1936–48 B ● 36B BENTLEY 2-SEATER SPORTS COUPE WITH DRIVER AND PASSENGER 1937–41 D

4th Row 24C TOWN SEDAN 1934–41 E ● 30B ROLLS-ROYCE CAR 1935–41 B

5th Row 30D VAUXHALL CAR 1935–41 D (repainted) ● 30A CHRYSLER 'AIRFLOW' SALOON 1934–41 E

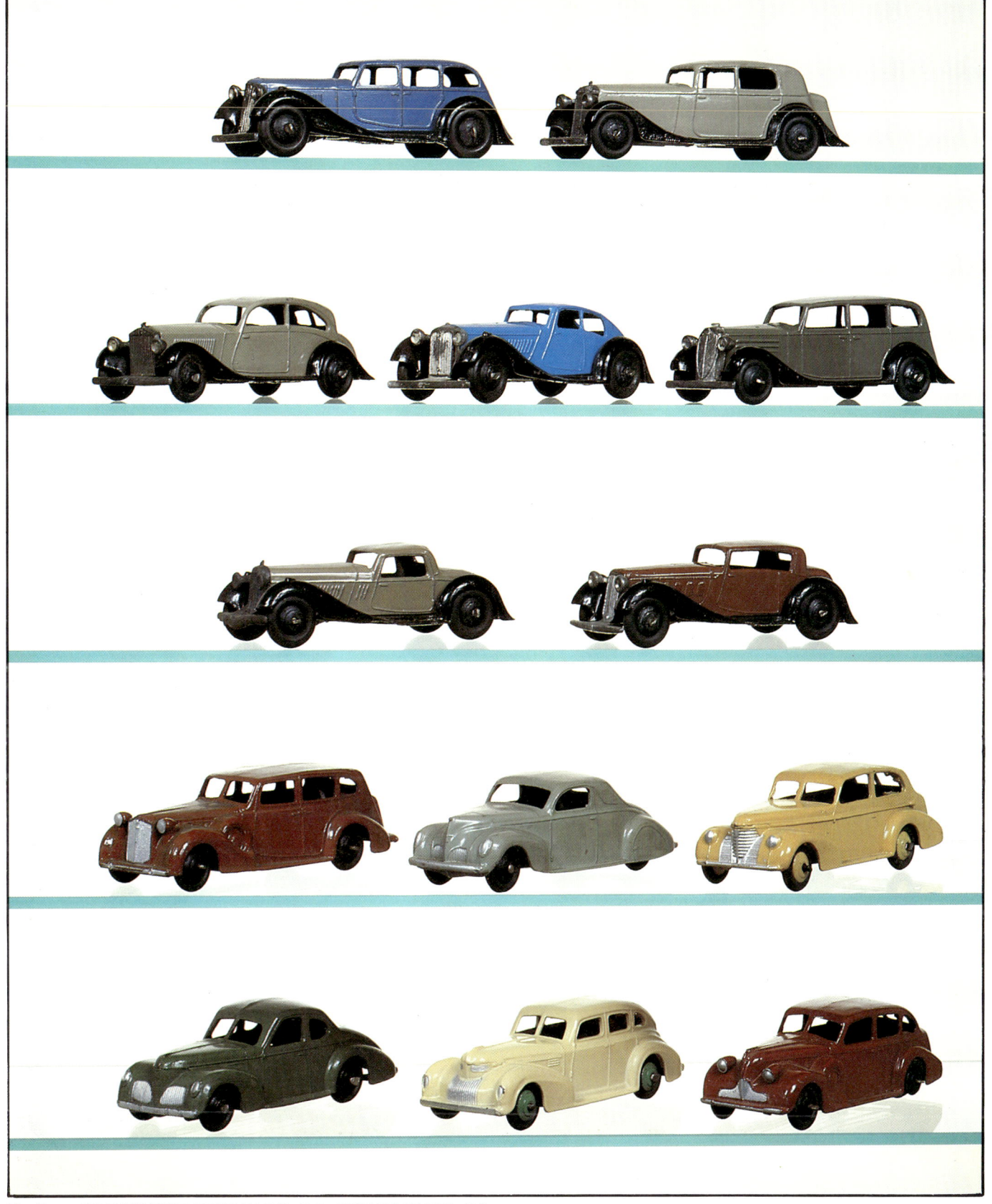

Top Row 36A ARMSTRONG-SIDDELEY 1946–48 C ● 30C DAIMLER 1946–48 C
2nd Row 30B ROLLS-ROYCE 1946–50 C ● 36D ROVER 1946–48 C ● 30D VAUXHALL 1946–48 C
3rd Row 36B BENTLEY 1946–48 C ● 36C HUMBER 1946–48 C
4th Row 39A PACKARD SUPER 8 1946–50 C ● 39C LINCOLN ZEPHYR 1946–50 C ● 39B OLDSMOBILE 6 1946–50 C
5th Row 39F STUDEBAKER STATE COMMANDER 1946–50 C ● 39E CHRYSLER ROYAL 1946–50 C ● 39D BUICK VICEROY 1946–50 C

Top Row 140B/156 ROVER 75 1951–56 B ● 40G/159 MORRIS OXFORD 1950–56 B ● 162 FORD ZEPHYR 1956–60 B
2nd Row 40E/153 STANDARD VANGUARD 1950–60 B ● 40B/151 TRIUMPH 1800 1948–60 B ● 40A/158 RILEY 1947–60 B
3rd Row 40F/154 HILLMAN MINX 1951–56 B ● 40D/152 AUSTIN DEVON 1949–56 B ● 164 VAUXHALL CRESTA 1957–60 B
4th Row 40J/161 AUSTIN SOMERSET 1954–56 B ● 161 AUSTIN SOMERSET 1956–60 B (152, 154, 156, and 159 were also 2-toned for this period) ● 162 FORD ZEPHYR 1956–60 B
5th Row 159 MORRIS OXFORD 1956–60 B ● 40E/153 STANDARD VANGUARD 1950–60 B ● 140B/156 ROVER 75 1951–56 B

DINKY AND CORGI 1950'S SALOON CARS

Top Row   DINKY 161 AUSTIN SOMERSET 1956–60 B ● CORGI 208S JAGUAR 2.4 LITRE 1960–63 B (as 208 without interior or suspension, 1957–60) ● CORGI 202 MORRIS COWLEY 1956–60 B

2nd Row   CORGI 216 AUSTIN A40 1959–62 B ● DINKY 183 FIAT 600 1958–60 B ● DINKY 152 AUSTIN DEVON 1956–60 B

3rd Row   CORGI 210 CITROËN DS19 1957–60 B (as 210S with interior and suspension 1960–65) ● CORGI 233 TROJAN HEINKEL BUBBLE CAR 1962–72 A ● CORGI 206 HILLMAN HUSKY 1956–60 B

4th Row   DINKY 154 HILLMAN MINX 1956–60 B ● CORGI 200 FORD CONSUL 1956–61 B ● DINKY 181 VOLKSWAGEN 1956–70 B

5th Row   DINKY 40A/158 RILEY 1947–60 B ● CORGI 203 VAUXHALL VELOX 1956–60 B ● DINKY 164 VAUXHALL CRESTA 1957–60 B

DINKY AMERICAN CARS OF THE 1950'S

Top Row 172 STUDEBAKER LAND CRUISER 1956–58 B ● 171 HUDSON COMMODORE 1956–58 B (as 139B or 171 with different 2-colour scheme 1950–56) ● 191 DODGE ROYAL SEDAN 1959–64 B
2nd Row 180 PACKARD CLIPPER 1958–63 B ● 172 STUDEBAKER LAND CRUISER 1954–56 B ● 178 PLYMOUTH PLAZA 1959–63 B
3rd Row 169 STUDEBAKER GOLDEN HAWK 1958–63 B ● 139A/170 FORD FORDOR 1949–56 B ● 177 PLYMOUTH PLAZA 1959–63 B
4th Row 179 STUDEBAKER PRESIDENT 1958–63 B ● 131 CADILLAC ELDORADO 1956–63 B ● 170 FORD FORDOR 1956–59 B
5th Row 191 DODGE ROYAL SEDAN 1959–64 B ● 172 STUDEBAKER LAND CRUISER 1956–58 B ● 132 PACKARD CONVERTIBLE 1955–61 B

DINKY AND CORGI AMERICAN CARS OF THE 1950'S AND 1960'S

Top Row   DINKY 148 FORD FAIRLANE 1962–66 B ● CORGI 214S FORD THUNDERBIRD HARDTOP 1962–65 B (as 214 without interior or suspension 1959–62) ● DINKY 174 HUDSON HORNET 1958–63 B

2nd Row   DINKY 147 CADILLAC 62 1962–69 B ● DINKY 173 NASH RAMBLER 1958–62 B

3rd Row   CORGI 248 CHEVROLET IMPALA 1965–67 B (as 220 without chromework 1960–65) ● CORGI 235 OLDSMOBILE 88 1962–66 B ● CORGI 229 CHEVROLET CORVAIR 1961–66 A

4th Row   DINKY 449 CHEVROLET EL CAMINO PICK-UP 1961–69 B ● CORGI 219 PLYMOUTH SPORTS SUBURBAN 1959–63 B (as 445 with suspension 1963–65)

5th Row   CORGI 211 STUDEBAKER GOLDEN HAWK 1958–60 B (as 211S with interior and suspension 1960–65) ● CORGI 325 FORD MUSTANG COMPETITION 1966–69 A ● CORGI 215S FORD THUNDERBIRD CONVERTIBLE 1962–65 B (as 215 without driver or suspension 1959–62)

DINKY SALOONS OF THE LATE 1950'S AND EARLY 1960'S

Top Row   155 FORD ANGLIA 1961–66 A ● 166 SUNBEAM RAPIER 1958–63 B ● 145 SINGER VOGUE 1962–67 B
2nd Row   189 TRIUMPH HERALD 1959–64 A ● 187 VOLKSWAGEN KARMANN-GHIA COUPE 1959–64 B ● 166 SUNBEAM RAPIER 1958–63 B
3rd Row   176 AUSTIN A105 1958–63 B ● 140 MORRIS 1100 1963–69 A ● 144 VOLKSWAGEN 1500 1963–67 A
4th Row   168 SINGER GAZELLE 1958–63 B ● 135 TRIUMPH 2000 1963–69 A ● 195 JAGUAR 3.4 LITRE MARK II 1960–66 B
5th Row   143 FORD CAPRI 1962–67 A ● 165 HUMBER HAWK 1959–63 B ● 177 OPEL KAPITAN 1961–66 A

DINKY AND CORGI 1960'S CARS

Top Row   DINKY 133 FORD CONSUL CORTINA 1965–69 A (as 139 with earlier grille 1963–65) ● DINKY 130 FORD CONSUL CORSAIR 1964–69 A ● CORGI 239 VOLKSWAGEN 1500 KARMANN-GHIA 1963–68 A

2nd Row   DINKY 186 MERCEDES-BENZ 220SE 1961–67 A ● CORGI 230/253 MERCEDES-BENZ 220SE COUPE 1962–68 A (230 has steering 1962–64) ● DINKY 138 HILLMAN IMP 1963–73 A

3rd Row   CORGI 224 BENTLEY CONTINENTAL SPORTS SALOON 1961–66 B ● DINKY 127 ROLLS-ROYCE SILVER CLOUD III 1964–72 B ● CORGI 224 BENTLEY CONTINENTAL SPORTS SALOON 1961–66 B

4th Row   CORGI 316 NSU SPORT PRINZ 1963–66 A ● CORGI 499 CITROËN ID19 '1968 OLYMPIC WINTER SPORTS' 1968–69 A (3 other liveries from 1963) ● CORGI 238 JAGUAR MARK X 1962–67 A

5th Row   CORGI 252 ROVER 2000 1963–66 A ● DINKY 194 BENTLEY 'S' SERIES COUPE 1964–67 B ● DINKY 162 TRIUMPH 1300 1966–70 A

SPOT-ON CARS

Top Row   401 VOLKSWAGEN 1500 VARIANT 1967 C ● 185 FIAT 500 1963–64 A ● 287 HILLMAN MINX 1965–67 B
2nd Row   289 MORRIS MINOR 1000 1965–67 C ● 267 MG 1100 1964–67 B ● 101 ARMSTRONG-SIDDELEY 'SAPPHIRE 236' 1959–62 B
3rd Row   260 THE ROYAL ROLLS ROYCE 1964–68 D
4th Row   193 NSU PRINZ 1963–67 A ● 131 GOGGOMOBIL SUPER 1960–65 B ● 218 JAGUAR MARK X 1963–64 B
5th Row   114 JAGUAR 3.4 LITRE 1960–63 C ● 195 VOLKSWAGEN RALLY CAR 1963–64 B ● 154 AUSTIN A40 1961–63 B

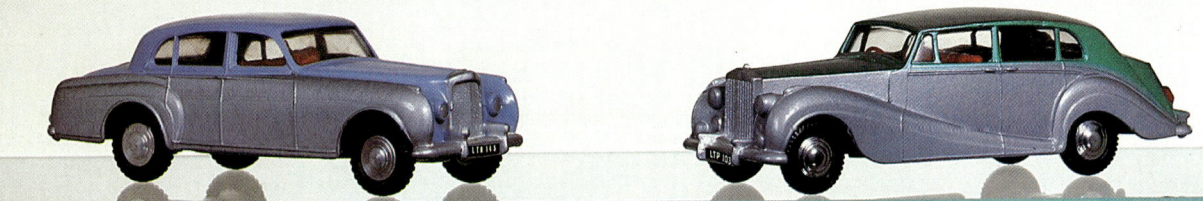

Top Row 115 BRISTOL 406 1960–62 C ● 193 NSU PRINZ 1963–67 A ● 405 VAUXHALL CRESTA PB 'BEA' 1966–67 B
2nd Row 216 VOLVO 122S 1963–64 B ● 213 FORD ANGLIA 1961–66 B ● 286 AUSTIN 1800 1965–67 B
3rd Row 102 BENTLEY SPORTS SALOON 1959–63 C ● 103 ROLLS ROYCE SILVER WRAITH 1959–62 D
4th Row 259 FORD CONSUL CLASSIC 1963–64 B ● 120 FIAT 600 MULTIPLA 1960–64 B ● 113 ASTON MARTIN DB3 1959–63 C
5th Row 280 VAUXHALL CRESTA PB 1965–67 B ● 274 MORRIS 1100 1965–67 B ● 100SL FORD ZODIAC 1961–63 B (battery-operated lights)

Top Row CORGI 317 MINI-COOPER 1964 MONTE CARLO 1964–65 A ● CORGI 340 MINI-MARCOS 850 1968–70 A ● CORGI 339 MINI-COOPER 1967 MONTE CARLO 1967–72 A ● DINKY 183 MORRIS MINI-MINOR 1966–75 A

2nd Row DINKY 197 MORRIS MINI-TRAVELLER 1961–70 A ● CORGI 334 MINI-MAGNIFIQUE 1968–70 A ● CORGI 226 MORRIS MINI-MINOR 1960–66 A ● CORGI 249 MORRIS MINI-COOPER WITH WICKERWORK 1965–68A

3rd Row SPOT-ON 210/1 MINI-VAN 'ROYAL MAIL' 1962–63 B ● CORGI 448 POLICE MINI-VAN 1964–69 A ● SPOT-ON 210/2 MINI-VAN 'GPO TELEPHONES' 1962–63 B

4th Row DINKY 274 AA PATROL MINI-VAN 1972–73 B (with earlier AA livery 1964–72) ● CORGI 450 AUSTIN MINI-VAN 1964–67 A ● CORGI 485 AUSTIN MINI-COUNTRYMAN 1965–71 A

5th Row CORGI 226 MORRIS MINI-MINOR 1966–71 A ● DINKY 342 AUSTIN MINI-MOKE 1966–75 A ● CORGI 226 MORRIS MINI-MINOR 1960–66 A ● DINKY 178 MINI CLUBMAN 1975–79 A

DINKY CARS OF THE LATE 1960'S AND EARLY 1970'S

Top Row 159 FORD CORTINA MK II 1967–70 A ● 169 FORD CORSAIR 2000E 1967–69 A ● 165 FORD CAPRI 1969–76 A
2nd Row 164 FORD ZODIAC MK 4 1966–71 A ● 136 VAUXHALL VIVA 1964–73 A ● 205 FORD CORTINA RALLY CAR 1968–73 A
3rd Row 188 JENSEN FF 1968–75 A ● 190 MONTEVERDI 375 L 1970–74 A ● 160 MERCEDES-BENZ 250SE 1967–74 A
4th Row 179 OPEL COMMODORE COUPE 1971–75 A ● 161 FORD MUSTANG FASTBACK 2+2 1965–73 A ● 176 NSU RO 80 1969–74 A
5th Row 149 CITROËN DYANE 1971–75 A ● 166 RENAULT 16 1967–70 A ● 154 FORD TAUNUS 17M 1966–69 A

SMALL-SCALE CARS OF THE LATE 1950'S AND EARLY 1960'S

Top Row MATCHBOX 53 ASTON MARTIN DB2 1958–63 A ● MATCHBOX 29 AUSTIN A55 CAMBRIDGE 1961–66 A ● MATCHBOX 33 FORD ZODIAC MK II 1957–61 A

2nd Row MATCHBOX 32 JAGUAR XK140 1957–62 A (unusual colour) ● MATCHBOX 46 MORRIS MINOR 1000 1958–60 B ● MATCHBOX 36 AUSTIN A50 CAMBRIDGE 1957–61 A

3rd Row MATCHBOX 39 PONTIAC CONVERTIBLE 1962–67 A (unusual colour) ● MATCHBOX 39 FORD ZODIAC II CONVERTIBLE 1957–62 A ● MATCHBOX 27 CADILLAC SIXTY SPECIAL 1960–66 A ● MATCHBOX 31 FORD FAIRLANE STATION WAGON 1960–64 A

4th Row CHARBENS OC.7 1898 PANHARD *ca* 1960 A ● CHARBENS OC.5 1907 VAUXHALL *ca* 1960 A ● CHARBENS OC.2 1904 SPYKER *ca* 1960 A ● CHARBENS OC.6 1902 DE DION BOUTON *ca* 1960 A

5th Row MATCHBOX MODELS OF YESTERYEAR Y10 1908 MERCEDES GRAND PRIX 1958–63 B ● MATCHBOX MODELS OF YESTERYEAR Y5 1929 BENTLEY 4½ LITRE LE MANS 1958–62 B

Fast and flashy
Sports cars and open tourers

The two cars in the original Modelled Miniatures 22 Series, later called Dinky Toys, were both sports cars: the Sports Coupé was modelled on William Lyons' SS1 (the letters stand for Swallow Sidecars), the forerunner of the famous Jaguar range, while the Sports Car was another Lyons design, a Swallow-bodied Standard or Wolseley. Being made of lead alloy, they do not suffer from the fatigue of later Dinkies, but the softer metal makes them more susceptible to play damage, and the Sports Car is extremely hard to find with its windscreen intact. These two are the most valuable of all Dinky cars.

Equally rare, but by no means as valuable, are two very similar models of the same cars by the small English Dyson firm. Although these are generally regarded as copies of the Dinky Toys, 50 years later it is difficult to determine which came first. Two open tourers, a two-seater and a four- seater, were included in the 24 Series. These had open, later filled-in tinplate windscreens and rear-mounted spare wheels. In their 36 Series guise they were named British Salmson, cast lead drivers were pegged into holes in the seats, and the four-seater lost its spare wheel. Post-war re-issues had neither spare wheels nor drivers, the holes in the seats having been filled in. The Streamlined Tourer, issued in 1935, was an open two-seater version of the smaller Chrysler Airflow saloon, although no such real car existed. The diminutive Austin Seven Ruby saloon was joined by a pretty Opal tourer in 1938, the pre-war version having a wire windscreen frame, and an MG Midget PA appeared in the same Small Cars set as the saloon. Finally, the Alvis, Sunbeam-Talbot and Frazer-Nash BMW from the important 38 Series Sports Cars appeared in 1940, these being joined by the Jaguar SS100 and Lagonda in 1946. The vulnerable front wings of the Jaguar make it the hardest to find in good condition.

The sixth member of the 38 Series was to have been a Triumph Dolomite Sports Coupé, but this was never made, and its place was taken by a model of the Armstrong-Siddeley Hurricane, issued in 1946 and constituting the first Dinky model of a post-war car.

The Dinky Toy Austin Atlantic Convertible made from 1951 to 1958 was an exceptional model for several reasons. It is the only Dinky to have the windscreen cast into the body, rather than the separate casting of the pre-war tourers or the flat plastic windscreens of the 38 Series and later sports cars; it has recessed rather than raised lines throughout, a feature not repeated on a Dinky until 1960; more bright-work than usual is picked out, while the dashboard detail even includes the radio! The model is particularly stunning in black with red seats and white tyres: again, these tyres were not used on any other Dinky of the period. It is a pity the real car was not as successful as the Dinky Toy!

Sports cars featured strongly among the new releases of the mid-1950's, the MG TF Midget, Jaguar XK120 and Porsche 356 being among the more desirable Dinkies of the period. Particularly striking is a model of the aerodynamic Bristol 450 Le Mans car. Open American cars started to appear at the same time, including a pink Cadillac! These were the first open cars to have fully-modelled rather than flat windscreens.

Sports cars and open American cars also featured in the Corgi, Morestone and Matchbox ranges in the late 1950's and early 1960's, but only two die-cast models were made of convertible versions of English cars, namely a Ford Zodiac by Matchbox and a Bentley 'S' Series by Dinky.

Plated versions of the Corgi Austin-Healey 100, Triumph TR2 and MGA were made in 1959. Mounted on black plastic plinths and called Trophy Models, they were sold exclusively in Marks and Spencer's shops.

Spot-On's sports cars included several not featured in other ranges, the Jaguar XKSS and Daimler SP250 Dart being two of the more interesting choices.

The exciting Jaguar E-Type was a very popular subject, no less than eight different die-cast models having been made in this country in the 1960's. Much the best of these are the two Corgi models – a Roadster issued in 1962 and a very detailed 2 + 2 Coupé issued in 1968. A much less detailed V-12 2 + 2 replaced the latter in the early 1970's.

Since the late 1960's, the accent has been firmly on 'foreign' sports cars such as Ferraris and Lamborghinis, a reflection of the decreasing demand for British sports cars, notable exceptions being Dinky's Triumph TR7 of 1976, the first TR since the Corgi and Spot-On TR3's of 1959/60 and the last $1/42$nd scale Dinky car, and Corgi's $1/36$th scale Jaguar XJS and Lotus Elite.

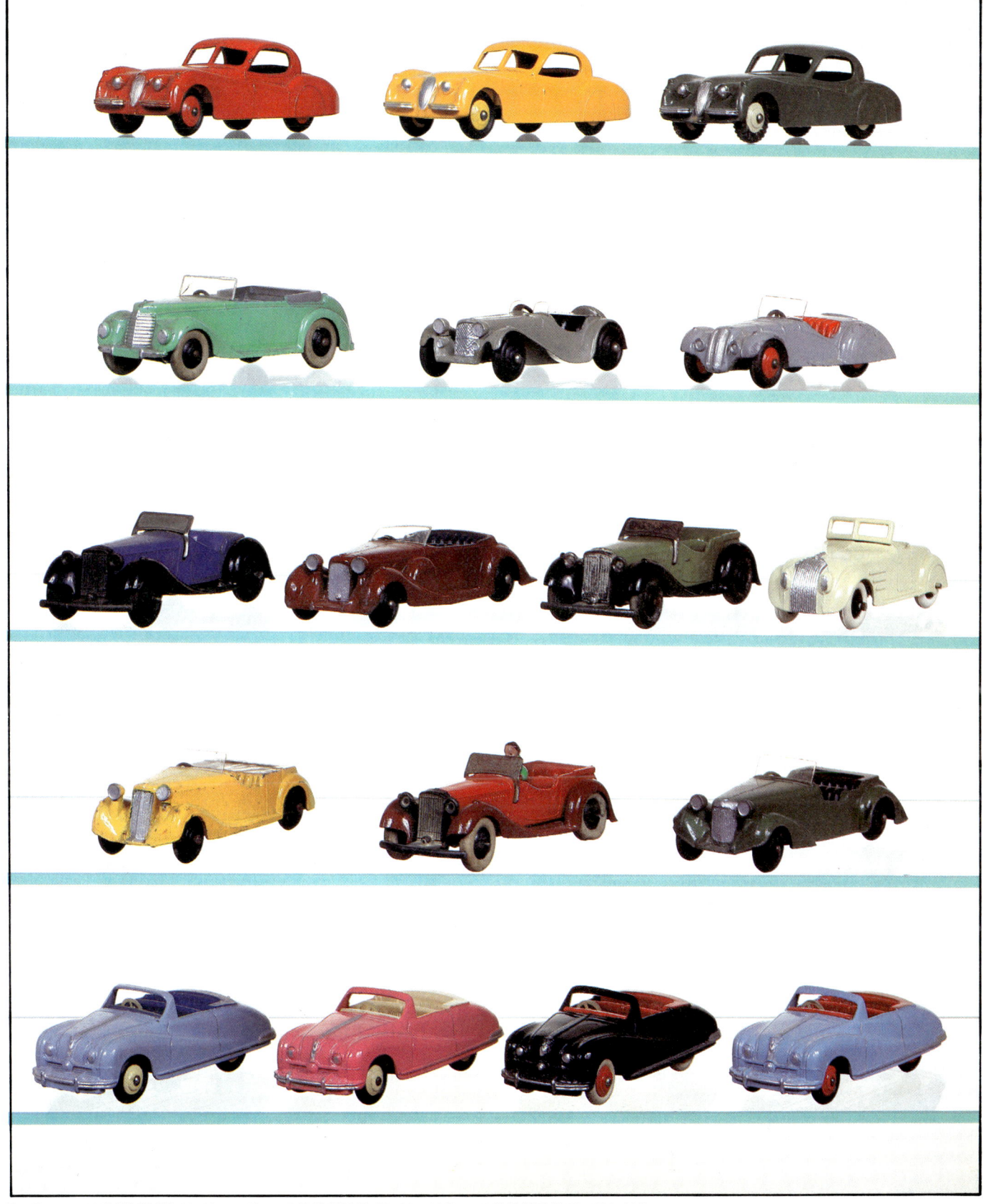

Top Row   157 JAGUAR XK120 1954–62 B ● 157 JAGUAR XK120 1954–62 B ● 157 JAGUAR XK120 1954–62 B
2nd Row   38E ARMSTRONG-SIDDELEY 'HURRICANE' 1946–50 B ● 38F JAGUAR SS 100 1946–50 B ● 38A FRAZER-NASH BMW 1946–50 B
3rd Row   36E BRITISH SALMSON 2-SEATER 1946–48 C ● 38C LAGONDA SPORTS COUPE 1946–50 B ● 36F BRITISH SALMSON 4-SEATER 1946–48 C ● 22G STREAMLINED TOURER 1935–41 D (repainted)
4th Row   38B SUNBEAM-TALBOT SPORTS 1946–50 B ● 36E BRITISH SALMSON 4-SEATER 1937–41 E ● 38D ALVIS SPORTS TOURER 1946–50 B
5th Row   140A AUSTIN ATLANTIC CONVERTIBLE 1951–54 B ● 140A AUSTIN ATLANTIC CONVERTIBLE 1951–54 B ● 106 AUSTIN ATLANTIC CONVERTIBLE 1954–58 B ● 106 AUSTIN ATLANTIC CONVERTIBLE 1954–58 B

Top Row CORGI 300 AUSTIN-HEALEY 100 1956–63 B ● DINKY 167 AC ACECA 1958–63 B ● CORGI 302 MGA 1957–65 B
2nd Row DINKY 157 JAGUAR XK120 1954–62 B ● CORGI 305 TRIUMPH TR3A 1960–64 B ● DINKY 103 AUSTIN-HEALEY 100 1957–60 B
3rd Row DINKY 106 AUSTIN ATLANTIC CONVERTIBLE 1954–58 B ● DINKY 157 JAGUAR XK120 1956–60 B
4th Row DINKY 101 SUNBEAM ALPINE 1957–60 B ● DINKY 167 AC ACECA 1958–63 B ● DINKY 105 TRIUMPH TR2 1957–62 B
5th Row DINKY 157 JAGUAR XK120 1954–62 B ● DINKY 238 JAGUAR 'D'-TYPE 1957–65 B ● DINKY 102 MG MIDGET TF 1957–60 B

DINKY AND CORGI SPORTS CARS OF THE 1960'S

Top Row DINKY 182 PORSCHE 356A COUPE 1958–66 B ● CORGI 324 MARCOS 1800GT 1966–69 A ● CORGI 319 LOTUS ELAN S2 HARDTOP 1967–68 A

2nd Row DINKY 185 ALFA ROMEO 1900 SUPER SPRINT 1961–63 B ● DINKY 112 AUSTIN -HEALEY SPRITE MK II 1961–66 B ● CORGI 307 JAGUAR 'E'-TYPE 1962–64 B

3rd Row CORGI 261 JAMES BOND'S ASTON MARTIN DB5 1966–68 A ● CORGI 335 JAGUAR 'E'-TYPE 2+2 1968–69 A

4th Row CORGI 303 MERCEDES-BENZ 300SL CONVERTIBLE 1958–61 A (as 303S with suspension 1961–66) ● CORGI 345 MGC GT 1968–69 A ● DINKY 113 MGB 1962–69 B

5th Row CORGI 258 THE SAINT'S VOLVO P1800 1965–69 A ● CORGI 304 MERCEDES-BENZ 300SL HARDTOP 1958–61 A (as 304S with suspension 1961–66) ● DINKY 114 TRIUMPH SPITFIRE 1963–71 A

SPOT-ON SPORTS CARS

Top Row   261 VOLVO P1800 1963–66 B (2nd version has opening bonnet only) ● 279 1934 MG PB MIDGET 1965–67 B ● 113 ASTON MARTIN DB3 1959–63 C
2nd Row   219 AUSTIN-HEALEY SPRITE MK II 1963–67 B ● 217 JAGUAR 'E'-TYPE 1963–65 B ● 215 DAIMLER SP250 1961–66 C
3rd Row   112 JENSEN 541 1960–62 C ● 191 SUNBEAM ALPINE HARDTOP 1962–66 B ● 278 MERCEDES-BENZ 230SL HARDTOP 1965–67 B
4th Row   105 AUSTIN-HEALEY 100-SIX 1959–63 C ● 166 RENAULT FLORIDE 1962–65 B ● 281 MG MIDGET MK II 1966–67 B
5th Row   104 MGA 1959–65 C ● 107 JAGUAR XKSS 1960–63 C ● 108 TRIUMPH TR3A 1960–64 C

DINKY AND CORGI SPORTS AND RACING CARS OF THE 1950'S

Top Row   DINKY 111 TRIUMPH TR2 1956–59 B ● DINKY 110 ASTON MARTIN DB3S 1956–59 B ● DINKY 110 ASTON MARTIN DB3S 1956–59 B

2nd Row   DINKY 236 CONNAUGHT 'B' TYPE STREAMLINED GRAND PRIX RACING CAR 1956–59 B ● DINKY 109 AUSTIN-HEALEY 100 1955–59 B ● DINKY 163 BRISTOL 450 LE MANS 1956–60 B

3rd Row   DINKY 133 CUNNINGHAM C5R SPORTS-RACING CAR 1955–60 B ● DINKY 237 MERCEDES-BENZ W196 STREAMLINED GRAND PRIX RACING CAR 1957–69 B

4th Row   DINKY 108 MG MIDGET TF 1955–59 B ● DINKY 108 MG MIDGET TF 1955–59 B ● DINKY 107 SUNBEAM ALPINE 1955–59 B

5th Row   CORGI 151 LOTUS XI LE MANS 1958–64 B ● DINKY 109 AUSTIN-HEALEY 100 1955–59 B ● DINKY 107 SUNBEAM ALPINE 1955–59 B

Built for speed
Racing and record cars

The three Johillco record cars constitute the firm's most important contribution, since they are the first true models to have originated in this country. The bodies are hollow-cast in the manner of lead figures, and each of the cars – Henry Segrave's Golden Arrow, Kaye Don's Silver Bullet and Malcolm Campbell's Bluebird II – is inscribed with the achievements of the real car, though curiously the name Johillco is omitted. The Silver Bullet is the scarcest of these excellent models, and is often missing its separately-cast tailfins. Tootsietoy had made a Bluebird I, but for some reason this was not copied.

The pre-war Dinky Toy racing cars are a strange selection. Meccano used the term 'racing car' very loosely, as most of the cars depicted were actually record cars. The first to appear, called simply Racing Car, was a lead model of George Eyston's MG Magic Midget. This was re-cast in mazak in late 1934, with driver's head and exhaust detail added, and in this version represents the six-cylinder MG Magnette. It was originally given the pretty striped humbug finish of the real car, but later the simpler paint scheme of the first version was employed. This was followed by another Eyston car, the Hotchkiss Montlhèry 48-hour record breaker, in 1935. A small MG 'R' Type racer was issued with the previously-mentioned Austin Ruby and MG PA in 1936. In the same year came three cars heavily influenced by the Märklin products of the period. They had tin-plate baseplates held in Märklin-style by crimps in the body (this method proved unsatisfactory, and post-war baseplates were rivetted in place) and were fitted with large Märklin-like black tyres with a herring-bone tread pattern. Finally, two of the models were of German cars – a Mercedes-Benz W25 racer, the only pre-war Dinky model of a Grand Prix car, and an Auto-Union record car, a fabulous example of '30's streamlining. The third model was another Eyston car, the Speed of the Wind 24-hour record breaker.

Yet another Eyston car followed in 1938, the 312 mph Thunderbolt Land Speed Record breaker. This was the first Dinky car to have an individual box, with details of the car on the lid. A cheaper, unboxed version in assorted colours, called Streamlined Racing Car (who would *race* a 71 litre monster?), followed in 1939. In the same year, a pretty model of Goldie Gardner's MG record car appeared, again with an individual box. This car also has an Eyston connection, for it was a re-bodied version of

his Humbug Magnette. All Dinky racing and record cars re-appeared after the war, but not the boxes, and the Racing Car, Speed of the Wind, Streamlined Racing Car and MG 'R' continued into the mid-1950's. The striped Humbug and the boxed Thunderbolt and MG are hard to find in good condition.

Two versions of Malcolm Campbell's Bluebird III record breaker were made by Britains in the mid-1930's. The first has a removable body revealing exquisite engine and transmission detail and came in a beautifully illustrated box. The second was a cheaper, one-piece model with no box and is now considerably rarer. Also rare is another excellent two-piece model of John Cobb's Railton record car, made up till the war.

A rather crude Charbens model of Bluebird III was one of the firm's few original pre-war models. The only pre-war English racing car model was the excellent ERA in the small series made by Scamold.

The six Dinky Grand Prix racers issued in the early 1950's, most of which stayed in production for over ten years, were some of the most popular toys of the era. Their play value is evidenced by the relative difficulty in finding good examples today. They were followed by some rather less successful models, including a streamlined Mercedes GP incorrectly finished in white.

A correctly-finished silver model of this car was included in the Crescent racing car series of the mid-1950's, which also featured the much-publicised but unsuccessful BRM V-16. The Crescent models are generally better than their Dinky equivalents, but were not nearly so popular at the time. The last in the series a Vanwall, is now the hardest to find.

Corgi's BRM and Vanwall were also given the 'Trophy' treatment. The firm also produced the only post-war die-cast record car, a model of Donald Campbell's Bluebird which was eventually to beat John Cobb's record of 1947.

Very few racing car models were made in the 1960's, the Corgi Lotus-Climax and Cooper-Maserati being the only notable ones. Large numbers of dragsters and hot rods followed the introduction of low-friction wheels in 1970. Larger scales were employed for Formula 1 cars in the 1970's: $1/32$nd scale in the case of Dinky, while the Surtees TS9B and McLaren M19A issued in 1972 were the first of the $1/36$th scale Corgi Toys.

RACING AND RECORD CARS OF THE 1930'S

Top Row DINKY 23C MERCEDES-BENZ W25 1946–50 B ● DINKY 23A/220 MG EX-135 MAGNETTE 1946–56 A ● DINKY 23E/221 SPEED OF THE WIND RECORD CAR 1946–57 A

2nd Row DINKY 23P GARDNER'S MG RECORD CAR 1946–48 B ● DINKY 23B HOTCHKISS RECORD CAR 1946–48 B ● DINKY 23P GARDNER'S MG RECORD CAR 1939–41 D

3rd Row BRITAINS 1400 MALCOLM CAMPBELL'S BLUEBIRD III 1935–40 E ● DINKY 23D AUTO-UNION RECORD CAR 1936–46 C (without driver 1947–50 B)

4th Row JOHILLCO 650 MALCOLM CAMPBELL'S BLUEBIRD II 1930'S D ● JOHILLCO 648 HENRY SEGRAVE'S GOLDEN ARROW 1930'S D

5th Row DINKY 23A MG EX-135 MAGNETTE 1935–41 B ● DINKY 23A MG EX-135 MAGNETTE 1935–41 B ● JOHILLCO 667 MAGIC MIDGET 1930'S B (called 'Flying Scud' in catalogue!)

Top Row **DINKY GIFT SET 4 RACING CARS 1953–58 D (renumbered 249 in 1954) CONTAINING:** 23G/233 COOPER-BRISTOL 1953–64 B ● 23F/232 ALFA ROMEO 1952–64 B ● 23H/234 FERRARI 1953–64 B ● 23J/235 HWM 1953–60 B ● 23N/231 MASERATI 1953–64 B

2nd Row CRESCENT 1286 FERRARI 2.5 LITRE GP 1957–60 B ● DINKY 23A/220 MG EX-135 MAGNETTE 1946–56 A ● DINKY 23K/230 TALBOT-LAGO 1953–64 B

3rd Row DINKY 239 VANWALL 1958–65 B ● CRESCENT 1289 GORDINI 2.5 LITRE GP 1957–60 B

Transports of delight
Buses, coaches and taxis

The distinctive shapes of British buses and coaches made it more important for the home manufacturers to produce original material, although Johillco did make a copy of the very American-looking Tootsietoy Fageol coach. The firm also made a model of a General double-decker and a quaint model of an open char-a-banc, which at 2 inches (50mm) long is one of the smallest Johillco vehicles.

T&B made a trolleybus in two sizes. The larger, 5 inch (125mm) version had sprung poles and a conducter on the rear step and is one of the most impressive T&B vehicles, and also one of the rarest. The 3½ inch (87mm) version was a much cruder, slush-cast effort and was re-issued post-war by Barrett and Sons (B&S). Also in the T&B range was a beautiful Streamline Coach, with attractive two-tone paintwork.

The first Dinky bus was a model of the very modern-looking Q-Type centre-entrance double-decker. Despite being only 2¾ inches (70mm) long, it is well detailed, and employed an unusual construction method for a Dinky, the cast chassis being held in place by tabs projecting from the body. This method was also used on the AEC double-decker issued in 1938 and made up till 1962, by which time it had acquired a Leyland grille. Strangely, only the very last issue was painted all-over red for the London market, while the pre-war version can be identified by the rudimentary stairs cast onto the rear platform.

A model of the Austin low-loader taxi appeared in 1938, one of the prettiest Dinky Toys of all time. Again, an unusual construction method was used, with a driver and luggage bay cast into the base-plate. This same pattern was employed for the post-war Austin FX3 taxi made in several bright colours through the 1950's before acquiring the more usual black finish of the real vehicle for a few years prior to its deletion in 1962. The small models of the FX3 in the Dinky-Dublo, Matchbox and Morestone ranges of the late 1950's all followed the construction pattern of the Dinky.

Of the Dinky coaches of the late 1940's and early '50's, none are truly representative, though the single deck bus or ½-cab has considerable period charm. The Matchbox Long Distance Coach was a good model of the SB, a typical mid-1950's coach. It came in two sizes, with 'London to Glasgow' transfers. Models of a London Transport trolley-bus and of the long-lived RT double-decker also featured in the Matchbox range.

A fine model of a Midland Red coach appeared in the Corgi range in the early 1960's and Spot-On did a good model of an ugly Mulliner-bodied coach at the same time. Both of these are now fairly scarce. The typical 1960's coach is represented by the large Dinky Vega Major, but the decade was dominated by models of the famous Routemaster double-decker, several of which are still available. The impressive Spot-On Routemaster is one of the more sought-after models in the range. Few models of later double-deckers have appeared, the single-entrance Dinky Leyland Atlantean and the Matchbox Daimler Fleetline being the only good ones.

Taxi versions of saloon cars are common in European die-cast ranges, but this trend was not repeated in Britain. One of the few exceptions is the Dinky Renault Dauphine Mini-Cab of the early 1960's, actually a borrowed French Dinky casting, plastered with advertisements in the fashion of the day. It is an improbable choice for a mini-cab. Not only is it a 'foreign' car, but it is rear-engined to boot!

Fewer models of the current Austin FX4 taxi have been made than of the Routemaster, the early Corgi offering being perhaps the best. The ghastly Dinky FX4 joined the many bus models painted silver for the Queen's Silver Jubilee in 1977. Simple but good models of the FX4 have recently appeared in the Budgie and Lone Star ranges for sale in London's souvenir shops.

Top Row DINKY 36G AUSTIN LOW LOADER 1938–40 C ● DINKY 36G AUSTIN LOW LOADER 1946–49 C ● DUBLO-DINKY 067 AUSTIN FX3 1959–67 B
2nd Row DINKY 40H/254 AUSTIN FX3 1951–56 B ● DINKY 254 AUSTIN FX3 1959–62 B
3rd Row CORGI 480 CHEVROLET IMPALA TAXI 1965–69 B (as 221 all yellow without chrome 1960–65) ● DINKY 266 PLYMOUTH PLAZA 'METRO CAB' 1960–66 B (for Canadian market only to 1965) ● DINKY 265 PLYMOUTH PLAZA USA TAXI 1960–66 B
4th Row CORGI 418 AUSTIN FX4 1960–74 A ● SPOT-ON 155 AUSTIN FX4 1961–62 B
5th Row DINKY 284 AUSTIN FX4 1972–80 A ● DINKY 241 AUSTIN FX4 'SILVER JUBILEE' 1977 A

DOUBLE-DECKER BUSES AND A TRAM

Top Row   DINKY 29 Q-TYPE CENTRAL-ENTRANCE BUS 1934–38 D ● MATCHBOX MODELS OF YESTERYEAR Y2 1911 'B' TYPE LONDON BUS 1956–63C ● MATCHBOX MODELS OF YESTERYEAR Y3 1907 LONDON 'E' CLASS TRAMCAR 1956–66 B ● MATCHBOX MODELS OF YESTERYEAR Y12 1899 LONDON HORSE-DRAWN BUS 1959–67 C

2nd Row   DINKY 29C DOUBLE DECK BUS 1949–54 B (the 2nd type AEC cab, as 290 with 'Dunlop' advertising 1954–59 C) ● DINKY 290 DOUBLE DECK BUS 'DUNLOP' 1957–63 C (the Leyland cab, as 29c without advertising 1948–54 A)

3rd Row   DINKY 29C DOUBLE DECK BUS 1946–48 B (the 1st AEC cab, with stairs and 'Dunlop' advertising 1938–41 D) ● DINKY 291 DOUBLE DECK BUS 'EXIDE' 1959–63 C ● DINKY 29C DOUBLE DECK BUS 1946–48 B

4th Row   DINKY 292 ATLANTEAN BUS 1962–63 C (with 'Regent' advertising 1963–65) ● DINKY 289 ROUTEMASTER LONDON BUS 'TERN SHIRTS' 1964–65 B ● DINKY 289 ROUTEMASTER LONDON BUS 'SCHWEPPES' 1965–69 B (with 'Esso' advertising 1970–80 A)

DOUBLE-DECKER BUSES

Top Row DINKY 290 LEYLAND DOUBLE-DECKER 'DUNLOP' 1957–63 C ● DINKY 29C AEC DOUBLE-DECKER 1946–49 B
2nd Row CORGI 468 ROUTEMASTER 1964–75 B ● BUDGIE 236 ROUTEMASTER 1962-CURRENT A (example shown has early transfer)
3rd Row DINKY 289 ROUTEMASTER 1970–80 A (issued 1964 with other advertisements B) ● DINKY 289 ROUTEMASTER 1972–75 B (this version only sold at Tussaud's)
4th Row DINKY 293 ATLANTEAN BUS 1963–68 C ● DINKY 292 ATLANTEAN BUS 1962–65 C
5th Row MATCHBOX KING SIZE K15 'THE LONDONER' BUS 1972-CURRENT A ● DINKY 297 ATLANTEAN CITY BUS 'SILVER JUBILEE' 1977 A

Top Row DINKY 29B STREAMLINE BUS 1947–50 B (Holland Coachcraft design adapted by Dinky. With open rear window and roof flash 1936–46 C) ● DINKY 29E ¹/₂-CAB COACH 1948–52 B

2nd Row DINKY 29G/281 LUXURY COACH 1951–59 C ● DINKY 29G/281 LUXURY COACH 1951–59 C ● DINKY 29G/281 LUXURY COACH 1951–59 C (three colours shown)

3rd Row DINKY 29F/280 OBSERVATION COACH 1950–60 C ● DINKY 29F/280 OBSERVATION COACH 1950–60 C

4th Row DINKY 29H/282 LEYLAND ROYAL TIGER DUPLE ROADMASTER 1952–60 B ● DINKY 283 BOAC COACH COMMER HARRINGTON 1956–63 C

5th Row DINKY 949 WAYNE SCHOOL BUS 1961–64 C

Top Row DINKY 952/954 VEGA MAJOR LUXURY COACH 1964–76 B (952 has flashing indicators)
2nd Row DINKY 953 CONTINENTAL TOURING COACH 1963–65 D
3rd Row DINKY 283 AEC MERLIN SINGLE DECK BUS 'RED ARROW' 1971–76 B
4th Row SPOT-ON 145 ROUTEMASTER 1961–63 E

Serving the people
Military, police and emergency vehicles

Emergency and military vehicles have long been popular subjects for children's toys, no doubt because small boys so love wars and disasters!

Perhaps the first die-cast vehicle made in this country, even pre-dating copies of Tootsietoy products, is a grey ambulance made by Taylor and Barrett in the early 1920's. At 4¼ inches (108mm) long, it is to a considerably larger scale than other T&B vehicles, and seems to have been a one-off model, rather than part of a series. In the 1930's, T&B made the largest range of emergency vehicles. Five different fire engines were made, most of which were issued in Home Office grey, as well as the more customary red. The most impressive of them all is the Turn-Table Fire Escape: the three-part escape can be raised and turned by handles, making this the most ingenious pre-war die-cast vehicle made in Britain.

Also in the T&B range was an item called Fire Engine Streamline, which was a fully-enclosed design. This same style was used for the only pre-war Dinky Toy fire appliance, which was more accurately modelled on a Merryweather design. It was available with or without tinplate firemen tabbed to the baseplate, the version with figures being now quite rare. The figureless version continued to be made until the early 1960's.

Again, only one ambulance was made in the Dinky range. Originally issued in the 24 Series (see Saloon Cars), it was later given a 36 Series baseplate, but for confusion's sake was numbered in the 30 Series! The rear windows were open at first, but were filled in shortly after the war. A slush-cast copy of this ambulance was made by Charbens, who also copied an American slush-cast ambulance with a man standing precariously on the rear step.

Very few police vehicles were made before the war. Britains made a police version of their open two-seater military Staff Car, while Johillco converted their copy of the Tootsietoy Federal Van and put two figures in the cab.

Military vehicles appeared in quantity in all ranges in the late 1930's. Britains had in fact been making military vehicles for some years in ¹/₃₂nd scale to match their soldiers. Most of these shared a slush-cast cab unit and die-cast chassis, to which was fitted different bodies to make a tipping lorry, ambulance, half-tracked lorry, etc. The pre-war Square Cab type had two opening cab doors, and the articulated low loader, Underslung Lorry is the most sought-after version today. A small range of cast lead military vehicles was made by Skybirds to accompany their ¹/₇₂nd scale aircraft kit, starting in the mid-1930's. Again, most of them had a common cowl/chassis casting.

A tank with revolving turret and rubber tracks featured in the first Modelled Miniatures Motor Vehicles set, and continued to be made as a Dinky Toy up till the war. All the other pre-war Dinky military items appeared in the years 1937–40, and most were re-issued after the war. Two that were not, and which are now the most valuable of the series, are the four-wheel and six-wheel searchlight trucks. Militarised versions of standard models appeared in other ranges during this period, for example the T&B Breakdown Truck was given a camouflage finish.

A large number of rather basic open fire engines were made in the 1940's and 1950's. Of these, only the small and attractive Matchbox Dennises merit the designation 'model'. On the other hand, very few models of more modern designs appeared. Dinky issued a Commer with extending ladder in 1952, and a Bedford Turntable Escape in 1957, both of which were made into the late 1960's.

Only one model was made of the 'classic' 1950's fire appliance, the fully-enclosed Dennis with wheeled escape, and this was by Benbros in the small-scale series. Unfortunately, no satisfactory provision was made for attaching the separate escape, so it is often missing.

In the same series, Benbros made two other 'classic' emergency vehicles of the period, the Daimler Ambulance and the Wolseley 6/80 Police Car. The Daimler was widely modelled, the Dinky Toy being the commonest, but the best rendition was by Morestone in the large-scale series. Morestone also made rather better models of the Wolseley in two sizes. With minor casting changes, all these Morestones were re-released as Budgie Toys in the 1960's, and the small Police Car was joined by a green Squad Car and Fire Car variants on the same casting.

With the exception of the Morestone and Benbros Wolseleys, police vehicles tended to be based on already-existing saloon car castings, for example the Crescent Jaguar referred to in the introduction also appeared in police guise, and this pattern was followed for all the Corgi emergency vehicles of the late 1950's. Police and Fire Chief cars were made on the Riley Pathfinder and Jaguar 2.4 Litre castings respectively, while the Bedford CA Dormobile appeared in ambulance and fire tender guises.

Britains continued its range of military vehicles immediately after the war, the cab unit for the lorries having changed to a 'round cab' design with one opening door. The Round Cab Underslung Lorry is particularly scarce. This was replaced in the mid-1950's by a Fordson cab unit, and from this time all Britains vehicles were based on particular prototypes rather than generic designs.

A large range of Dinky military vehicles commenced in 1954, culminating in the Missile Erector Vehicle and Corporal Missile in 1960. A larger and more detailed model of this vehicle was issued in the Corgi Rocket Age range, which included RAF as well as army vehicles. Military models also appeared in the Matchbox range in the late 1950's.

From about 1960, many of the emergency vehicles in the Dinky, Corgi and Matchbox ranges were modelled on American subjects. Dinky, for example, converted no fewer than five of its American saloons into police cars between 1960 and 1970, and three of these were also made in Canadian RCMP livery. Flashing lights featured on the Dinky and Corgi Superior Ambulances in 1962, these being based on a Pontiac and Cadillac respectively. This feature was fitted to several other emergency vehicles in this period, the last being yet another Superior Ambulance, the Dinky Cadillac of 1967–71. The finest piece of the period is the magnificent American La France Ladder Truck by Corgi, issued in 1968 and made for nearly 15 years.

A number of Corgi models were painted in U S Army drab in the mid-1960's. The choice of models to be given this treatment was not good, some of them being too English to be realistic, even taking U S bases in Europe into account, and the series was short-lived.

Of the models of British emergency vehicles, the Spot-On Wadhams Ambulance and Jaguar Police Car should be mentioned since they are among the scarcer Spot-Ons. The BMC Wadhams was a popular custom-built ambulance in the 1960's, as was the Bedford Lomas modelled by Matchbox. The Jaguar was also issued in white to represent a motorway police car, a treatment also given to the Dinky Jaguar 3.4 Litre and Corgi Ford Zephyr Estate. Also in the Spot-On range was a white Ford Zephyr III from the 'Z-Cars' TV police series. The Dinky Humber Hawk Police Car is interesting in this respect in that it bears the registration number 'PC 49', one of the characters in the famous *Eagle* comic.

Several of the Corgi police vehicles of the 1960's and 1970's were issued in other liveries for specific European markets, for example in white with 'Politie' markings for the Dutch market. In the same way, most of the Dinky fire appliances and rescue vehicles of the 1970's were finished in 'Falck' livery for the Danish market. This was Dinky's most prolific period as far as fire appliances is concerned, and some of them were quite ingenious, with such features as operating water pumps or hose rewinding mechanisms. One of the last Dinky Toys to be made in this country was a fine model of an ERF Fire Tender.

A further large series of Dinky military vehicles to various specified scales was launched in the early 1970's. The Land Rover Bomb Disposal Unit had a particular relevance to the home market, but was actually quite short-lived.

Over the years, considerably fewer RAC vehicles have been issued than AA vehicles, presumably because the AA livery of yellow and black is more striking, and those that do exist are generally scarcer than their AA equivalents. Morestone made an AA Land Rover in three sizes in the 1950's, and models very similar to the smallest and largest of them were made by Benbros shortly afterwards. The Corgi Bedford CA van was used for an AA Road Service vehicle, and was accompanied by a Radio Rescue RAC Land Rover. Yet another Land Rover casting appeared in the Budgie range in the early 1960's in both AA and RAC liveries, while the rarest of these service vehicles are the AA and RAC Mini-vans in the Zebra Toys range. A Mini-van was also the choice for Dinky's belated entry into this field, and again appeared in both liveries.

POLICE VEHICLES

Top Row   CORGI 209 RILEY PATHFINDER 1958–61 B ● DINKY 256 HUMBER HAWK 1960–64 B
2nd Row   DINKY 250 MINI COOPER 'S' 1967–75 A ● DINKY 255 MINI CLUBMAN 1977–79 A ● CORGI 448 AUSTIN MINI-VAN 1964–69 A
3rd Row   DINKY 269 JAGUAR 3.4 LITRE MOTORWAY POLICE 1962–65 B ● DINKY 255 MERSEY TUNNEL POLICE LAND ROVER 1955–61 B ● CORGI 419 FORD
               ZEPHYR II ESTATE MOTORWAY POLICE 1960–65 B
4th Row   CORGI 223 CHEVROLET IMPALA STATE PATROL 1959–65 A ● CORGI 481 CHEVROLET IMPALA POLICE PATROL 1965–69 A
5th Row   DINKY 258 CADILLAC 62 USA POLICE 1966–68 B ● DINKY 264 CADILLAC 62 RCMP 1966–68 B ● DINKY 258 FORD FAIRLANE USA POLICE 1962–66 B

AMBULANCES

Top Row   DINKY 30H/253 DAIMLER 1950–60 B ● DINKY 253 DAIMLER 1960–66 B ● DINKY 30F AMBULANCE 1947–48 C (issued with open rear windows 1934–46)

2nd Row   CORGI 463 COMMER ¾-TON 1964–66 A ● DINKY 278 VAUXHALL VICTOR ESTATE 1964–68 B ● CORGI 412 BEDFORD CA UTILECON 1957–60 B (with single-piece windscreen 1960–61)

3rd Row   SPOT-ON 207 BMC WADHAMS 1961–64 D ● DINKY 263 PONTIAC SUPERIOR CRITERION 1962–68 A

4th Row   CORGI 437 CADILLAC SUPERIOR 1962–68 A ● CORGI 437 CADILLAC SUPERIOR 1962–68 A

5th Row   DINKY 276 FORD TRANSIT 1976–78 A (as 274 with revised grille 1978–80) ● DINKY 267 CADILLAC SUPERIOR 1967–71 A (without working lights as 288 1971–79)

FIRE ENGINES

Top Row DINKY 25K STREAMLINED FIRE ENGINE WITH FIREMEN 1937–39 E (as 25H/250 without firemen 1936–62 B) ● TAYLOR AND BARRETT FIRE ENGINE 1930'S D ● TAYLOR AND BARRETT STREAMLINE FIRE ENGINE 1930'S D

2nd Row CORGI 423 BEDFORD UTILECON FIRE TENDER 1960–62 B ● CORGI 405 BEDFORD UTILECON AFS TENDER 1956–60 B ● CHARBENS 1950'S A (missing the ladder)

3rd Row DINKY 555/955 COMMER EXTENDING LADDER 1952–60 B (with windows 1960–69) ● MODERN PRODUCT/MORESTONE 1950'S B ● DCMT CRESCENT 1950'S B

4th Row CORGI 1127 BEDFORD TK SIMON SNORKEL 1964–76 B ● MATCHBOX KING SIZE K15 AEC MERRYWEATHER TURNTABLE ESCAPE 1963–70 A

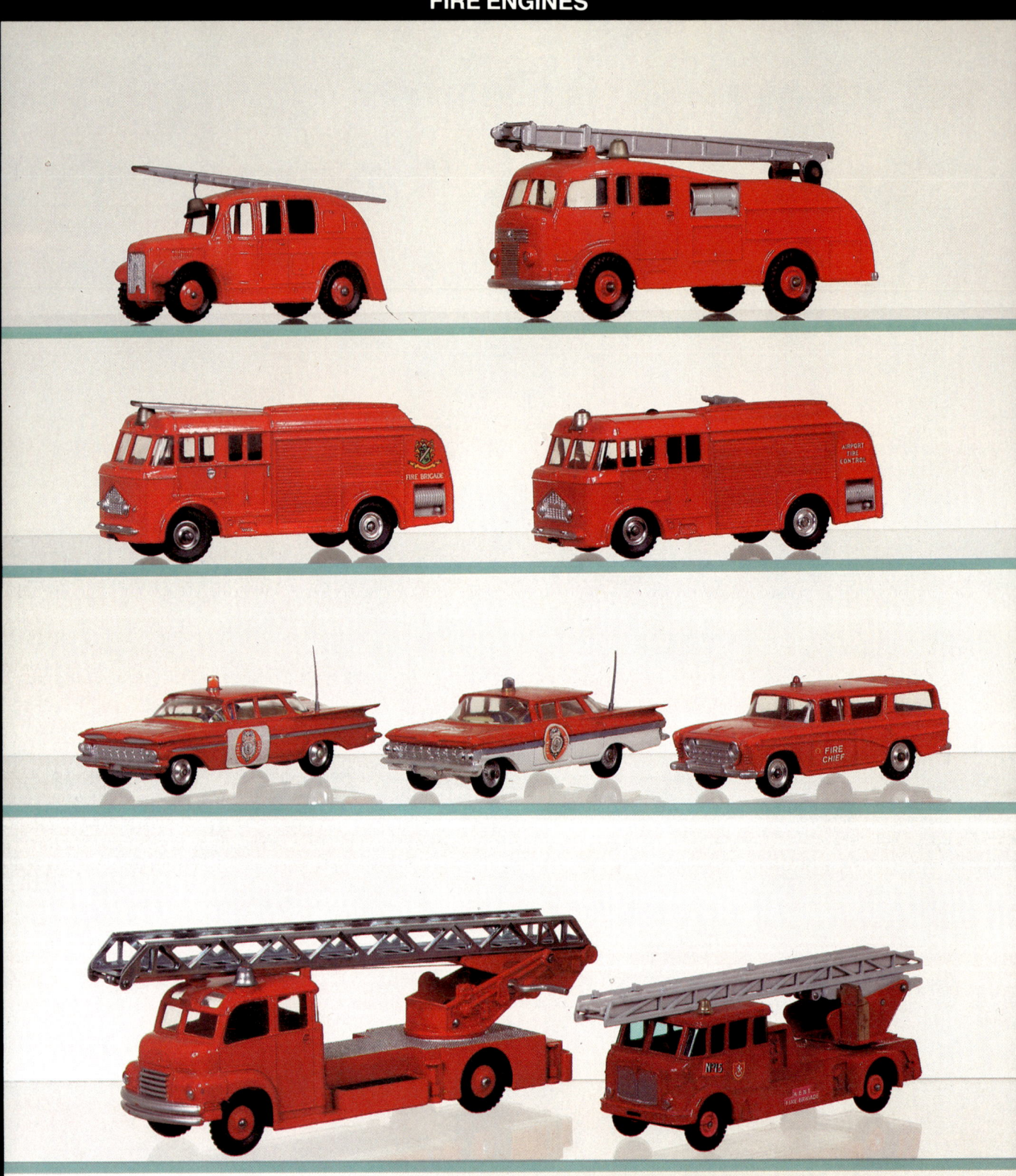

Top Row DINKY 250 STREAMLINED FIRE ENGINE 1954–62 B ● DINKY 955 COMMER EXTENDING LADDER 1960–69 B
2nd Row DINKY 259 BEDFORD FIRE TENDER 1961–69 B ● DINKY 276 BEDFORD AIRPORT FIRE TENDER 1962–69 B
3rd Row CORGI 439 CHEVROLET IMPALA FIRE CHIEF 1963–65 A ● CORGI 482 CHEVROLET IMPALA FIRE CHIEF 1965–69 A ● DINKY 257 NASH RAMBLER CANADIAN FIRE CHIEF 1961–68 B
4th Row DINKY 956 BEDFORD TURNTABLE ESCAPE 1958–60 B (with windows 1960–69) ● MATCHBOX KING SIZE K15 AEC MERRYWEATHER TURNTABLE ESCAPE 1963–70 A

Top Row DINKY 25Y/405 UNIVERSAL JEEP 1952–67 A ● DINKY 25J JEEP 1947–48 B ● DINKY 27D/340 LAND ROVER 1950–71 A

2nd Row SPOT-ON 161 LAND ROVER 109″W/B ESTATE CAR 1961–64 B ● SPOT-ON 308 LAND ROVER 109″W/B PICK-UP 1965–67 B (supplied with a trailer)

3rd Row SPOT-ON 415 LAND ROVER PICK-UP RAF FIRE SERVICE 1966–67 B ● CORGI 438 LAND ROVER PICK-UP 1962–77 A ● CORGI 416 LAND ROVER PICK-UP
RAC RADIO RESCUE 1959–62 B (as 416S with casting of 438 1962–64)

4th Row **CORGI GIFT SET 17 LAND ROVER WITH FERRARI RACING CAR ON TRAILER 1963–67 B CONTAINING:** 438 LAND ROVER AND 154 FERRARI F1 1963–71 A

5th Row DINKY 344 LAND ROVER PICK-UP 1970–79 A ● DINKY 192 RANGE ROVER 1970–69 A

Top Row MATCHBOX MODELS OF YESTERYEAR Y9, FOWLER 'BIG LION' SHOWMAN'S ENGINE 1958–68 C ● MATCHBOX MODELS OF YESTERYEAR Y11, 1920 AVELING AND PORTER STEAM ROLLER 1958–64 C ● MATCHBOX MODELS OF YESTERYEAR Y1, 1925 ALLCHIN TRACTION ENGINE, 1956–64 C

2nd Row MATCHBOX MODELS OF YESTERYEAR Y4, 1905 SHAND-MASON HORSE DRAWN FIRE ENGINE 1960–66 C ● MATCHBOX 9 DENNIS FIRE ENGINE 1955–58 B (1st of 2 similar models) ● MATCHBOX 7 HORSE-DRAWN MILK FLOAT 1954–61 B

3rd Row MATCHBOX 22 VAUXHALL CRESTA 1956–58 A ● MATCHBOX 74 MOBILE REFRESHMENTS CANTEEN 1959–66 A (unusual colour) ● MATCHBOX 21 COMMER MILK FLOAT 1961–68 A (an unusual door transfer)

4th Row MATCHBOX 18 CATERPILLAR BULLDOZER 1961–64 A (3rd of 4 similar models) ● MATCHBOX 28 FORD THAMES COMPRESSOR LORRY 1959–64 A ● MATCHBOX 38 KARRIER REFUSE WAGON 1957–63 A (unusual colour) ● MATCHBOX 26 ERF CEMENT MIXER 1956–61 A

5th Row MATCHBOX 56 LONDON TROLLEYBUS 1958–65 B ● MATCHBOX 21 BEDFORD SB DUPLE COACH 1958–61 A (2nd of 2 similar models) ● MATCHBOX 58 AEC PARK ROYAL BEA COACH 1958–62 A ● DUBLO-DINKY 067 AUSTIN FX3 TAXI 1959–67 B

DINKY MILITARY VEHICLES

Top Row **151 ROYAL TANK CORPS MEDIUM TANK SET 1938–41 E CONTAINING:** 151A MEDIUM TANK C ● 151B TRANSPORT WAGON B (re-issued after the war: *see below*) ● 151C COOKER TRAILER WITH STAND B ● 151D WATER TANK TRAILER B

2nd Row 151B 6-WHEELED TRANSPORT WAGON 1946–48 B ● **162 18-POUNDER QUICK FIRING FIELD UNIT 1939–48 C CONTAINING:** 162A LIGHT DRAGON MOTOR TRACTOR A ● 162B AMMUNITION TRAILER A ● 162C 18-POUNDER GUN A

3rd Row **161 MOBILE ANTI-AIRCRAFT UNIT 1939–41 D TO E (depending on state of metal) CONTAINING:** 161A SEARCHLIGHT LORRY D ● 161B AA GUN ON TRAILER A ● 37C ROYAL CORPS OF SIGNALS DESPATCH RIDER 1938–41 B

4th Row 665 'HONEST JOHN' MISSILE LAUNCHER 1964–76 B ● 667 INTERNATIONAL 6×6 MISSILE SERVICING PLATFORM VEHICLE 1960–61 C

DINKY MILITARY VEHICLES

Top Row 152B RECONNAISSANCE CAR 1938–48 B ● 153A JEEP 1946–48 B ● 674 AUSTIN CHAMP 1954–71 A
2nd Row 670 DAIMLER ARMOURED CAR 1954–71 A ● 688 MORRIS FIELD ARTILLERY TRACTOR 1957–71 A ● 673 DAIMLER SCOUT CAR 1954–62 A
3rd Row 621 BEDFORD RL 3-TON ARMY WAGON 1954–63 A ● 623 BEDFORD QL ARMY WAGON 1954–63 A ● 641 HUMBER 1-TON CARGO TRUCK 1954–62A
4th Row 676 ARMOURED PERSONNEL CARRIER 1955–62 A ● 651 CENTURION TANK 1954–71 A
5th Row 660 THORNEYCROFT 'MIGHTY ANTAR' TANK TRANSPORTER 1956–64 B (651 with 660 is 698 Tank and Transporter Gift Set 1957–65 B)

Top Row 661 SCAMMELL RECOVERY TRACTOR 1957–66 B ● 620 BERLIET MISSILE LAUNCHER 1971–73 A
2nd Row 30SM/625 AUSTIN COVERED WAGON 1950's C (US market only) ● 692 5.5" MEDIUM GUN 1955–62 A
3rd Row 642 RAF PRESSURE REFUELLER 1957–62 B ● 622 FODEN 10-TON ARMY TRUCK 1954–63 B
4th Row **695 HOWITZER AND TRACTOR SET 1962–66 C CONTAINING:** 689 LEYLAND MEDIUM ARTILLERY TRACTOR 1957–66 B ● 693 7.2" HOWITZER 1958–67 A
5th Row 677 ARMOURED COMMAND VEHICLE 1957–62 B ● 643 AUSTIN WATER TANKER 1958–64 A

CORGI MILITARY VEHICLES

Top Row GIFT SET 3 RAF LAND ROVER AND 'THUNDERBIRD' MISSILE ON TRAILER 1958–63 B CONTAINING: 350 THUNDERBIRD GUIDED MISSILE ON TOWING TROLLEY 1958–62 A ● 351 RAF LAND ROVER 1958–63 A

2nd Row 358 OLDSMOBILE SUPER 88 US ARMY STAFF CAR 1964–66 A ● 352 STANDARD VANGUARD PHASE III RAF STAFF CAR 1958–61 A

3rd Row 357 LAND ROVER WEAPONS CARRIER 1964–66 A ● 355 COMMER ¾-TON MILITARY POLICE VAN 1964–65 A ● 356 VOLKSWAGEN KOMBI US ARMY PERSONNEL CARRIER 1964–66 A

4th Row 1113 CORPORAL GUIDED MISSILE ON ERECTOR VEHICLE 1959–62 C

MILITARY VEHICLES

Top Row   CORGI 359 KARRIER ARMY FIELD KITCHEN 1964–66 A ● SPOT-ON 417 BEDFORD CA MILITARY FIELD KITCHEN 1966–67 B (both of these models originated as Ice Cream vans!)

2nd Row   DINKY 139AM/170M/675 FORD FORDOR U S ARMY STAFF CAR *ca* 1950–60 C (U S market only) ● CORGI 1133 INTERNATIONAL 6×6 TROOP CARRIER 1963–65 B (as 1118 without markings 1959–63)

3rd Row   DINKY 626 FORDSON MILITARY AMBULANCE 1956–66 B ● CORGI 414 BEDFORD CA UTILECON MILITARY AMBULANCE 1960–63 A ● CORGI 354 COMMER ¾-TON MILITARY AMBULANCE 1964–66 A

4th Row   DINKY 666 MISSILE ERECTOR VEHICLE AND 'CORPORAL' MISSILE 1959–64 C

Carry that load
Freight and goods vehicles

The Ford Model T pick-up is the earliest Tootsietoy to have been copied in England, in this case by Johillco from about 1930. The exterior detail is fairly basic, yet the buttoned upholstery and floorboard pattern is neatly portrayed. Johillco also copied the Federal Van, but unlike the Tootsietoy this does not carry lettering. The commonest of the copies are the Johillco and Charbens Mack Bulldog trucks. Most of the separate rears were similar to the Tootsie versions, but the Johillco Mail Van was an original design.

The Motor Truck and Delivery Van from the Modelled Miniatures 22 Series have a common cab and chassis unit with a tinplate grille surround. They may have been based on a Morris, although, as was usual with early Dinky Toys, they were not identified as such. Indeed, pre-war Dinky commercial vehicles are generally less readily identifiable than the cars, most being strictly generic types. The truck had an open rear with slatted sides, while the van had a flush-fitting rear held by a tinplate clip to the cab roof. This did not carry advertising at first, but with the introduction of the 28 Series vans in 1934, which used the same casting, the 22 Series van had 'Meccano' transfers.

In all, 13 different transfers appeared on this casting between 1934 and 1935, and these are the most valuable individual vehicles in the Dinky Toy range, and arguably the most attractive. Fortunately, they are made of lead alloy, and do not suffer from the fatigue of their successors.

The second type of 28 Series van was a one-piece mazak casting and is again a generic type; the grille bears a strong resemblance to a Ford 'Y' Type, but the rear has much smoother lines than any full-size Ford. Over 30 different transfers were used on this casting between 1935 and 1939, including at least two promotional issues, one of which was for a shop in Amsterdam. Needless to say, the promotional issues are very rare nowadays, while the high incidence of fatigue makes totally solid examples of any of the vans virtually impossible to find.

The third and last casting used for the 28 Series is now the hardest to find in *any* condition, having been made for at most two years during Dinky's worst period as far as metal quality is concerned. The grille is of an egg-box pattern similar to a Bedford of the period, but again the rear is a freelance design. The casting reappeared after the war, being made as a loud-speaker van until the mid-1950's, but never carried advertising.

Introduced at the same time as the first 28 Series Vans, the 25 Series Commercial Vehicles underwent fewer major changes in their long production life. There were six basic designs, all but the Petrol Tanker having the same cab styling. They were originally fitted with tin-plate radiator grilles, but these were replaced by cast grilles with headlamps in 1935–36, and no further changes were made in the body castings. The separately-cast chassis had three pear-shaped holes which were filled in shortly after the war. Finally, a totally new chassis appeared in 1948 which was used up till the series' deletion in 1950, having a front bumper and transmission detail cast in. A small selection of transfers appeared on the Covered Wagon in the pre-war years, and the Petrol Tanker appeared in eight different liveries. The last of these was a drab grey tanker with 'Pool' stencilled in white, which was issued in 1940 and briefly in 1946. 'Pool' was, as the name implies, a blended petrol – the only one available to war-time motorists. A trailer was made in colours to match the Flat Truck.

The few other pre-war Dinky commercial vehicles were more accurately based on real vehicles. A little Scammel three-wheeled Mechanical Horse with assorted trailers appeared in 1935. Many of the Petrol Tank and Box Van trailers were liveried, and attractive matching tugs and box van trailers were made in the liveries of the four railway companies. Being made of tinplate, these trailers tend to survive in good condtion, though the bases and tugs unfortunately do not. The Tug and Open Trailer were made after the war for many years.

The strange and rather attractive Royal Air Mail Service Car also appeared in 1935, actually predating the more traditional Royal Mail Van by three years. The real vehicles had the same Morris chassis, the Air Mail Car having a streamlined and totally impractical body which was used briefly by the Post Office to promote the new service. Only the Royal Mail Van was re-issued after the war; and the Air Mail Car is very hard to find in good condition. The Air Mail Car was also the subject for one of the few prototypical T & B vehicles issued.

Another one-off design was the Holland Coachcraft Van, a very streamlined design on a Bedford chassis. This model had a very short production run, and is consequently perhaps the rarest Dinky vehicle. A small number were cast in lead and these are the only fatigue-free examples known today. The casting was adapted to the much commoner Streamline Bus. Another interesting commercial from this period is the three-wheeled Thompson Aircraft Refuelling Tender issued in 1938 and pre-dated slightly by a rather simpler Skybirds model of the same vehicle.

The big event of 1947 was the launch of the Dinky Supertoys range, the first large commercial vehicles to be made to the same scale as the cars. Two chassis were used, each with a variety of bodies, an eight-wheeled Foden and a four-wheeled Guy Otter. The Foden cab originally had an upright rectangular grille, and the last body to be fitted, in 1952, was a flat truck with chains. This is now the scarcest of the first-type Fodens, for in the same year the cab was completely re-styled. Liveried Foden tankers first appeared in the following year, and the last Foden to be issued was a handsome Regent Tanker. Finally the open wagon, tanker and chain truck bodies were fitted to a Leyland Octopus chassis between 1958 and 1964, the last-mentioned being the hardest to find.

Van bodies in six different liveries were fitted to the Guy chassis in the 1950's, and these are now the most collected of post-war Dinky Toys. The same body, with 'Heinz' transfers, was fitted to a Guy Warrior chassis in 1960, and this is the most valuable of the vans. The livery had previously been applied to a Bedford van with two different transfers, the one with ketchup bottle being the scarcer.

Replacements for the 25 Series Trucks appeared in the late 1940's. The same six body styles were used, but with identifiable cabs. The proportions were the same as for the 25 Series. Some parts were re-used, for example the tinplate tilt for the Austin Covered Wagon and the tailgate for the Dodge Tipper. Again, the tanker was the odd-man-out, being based on an American rather than a British design. The 25 Series trailer was repainted in colours to match the Fordson Flat Truck.

Several small series of vans with advertising appeared through the 1950's, these pieces are very valuable today, the Trojan 'Oxo' and Morris 'Capstan' vans being the hardest to find. This latter model started life as a Royal Mail Van and has grilles on the rear windows. Its companion was a pretty Morris Post Office Telephone Van. Shortly afterwards, a Royal Mail Van appeared in the Dublo-Dinky range, which bears mentioning as it is the *only* die-cast model of the Morris Minor van.

Corgi's ingenuity in the early years is most evident in the Bedford 'S' articulated lorries in the Major range, Corgi's answer to Supertoys. The Car Transporter was a more satisfying toy than contemporary Dinky transporters. It featured simulated hydraulic ramps, while working winches were fitted to the machinery carriers, an idea borrowed from an excellent Crescent series of Scammel Mechanical Horses and Trailers. Several vans with advertising were made in this period, mostly on the Bedford CA castings, the most attractive being an ERF in 'Moorhouses' livery.

The Ecurie Ecosse Racing Car Transporter introduced in 1961 was one of the most detailed toys of its day, with steerable wheels and an opening door revealing a fully-equipped workshop.

Even more detailed was the American Ford H Tractor Unit introduced in the mid-1960's, with tilting cab and swivelling wing mirrors. This tractor was adapted as a Holmes Wrecker (breakdown truck), one of the finest toys ever in terms of play value. Successive Corgi commercials have been as well-proportioned, but not as detailed.

Being to $1/42$nd scale, the Spot-On commercial vehicles of the early 1960's are impressive models, and were the first to be fitted with interiors. The coupling mechanism on the articulated lorries is well executed; again the principle was borrowed from the Crescent Scammel. The liveried Petrol Tankers are the most desirable models in the range.

Very few advertising vans were made in the 1960's and 1970's in comparison with previous decades. Curiously, enough Dinky's last van, the Bedford CF, was only available in toy shops as a Royal Mail van, but several factory-prepared promotional issues were made on this casting.

PRE-WAR DINKY VANS

Top Row   28C DELIVERY VAN 'MANCHESTER GUARDIAN' 1934–35 E* (the 1st type of 28 Series van) ● 28B DELIVERY VAN 'PICKFORDS' 1934–35 E* (unusual wheels) ●
34B MORRIS ROYAL MAIL VAN 1938–48 B

2nd Row   28Y DELIVERY VAN 'EXIDE/DRYDEX' 1935–39 E (the 2nd type of 28 Series van) ● 28X DELIVERY VAN 'HOVIS' 1936–39 D ● 28 G DELIVERY VAN 'KODAK'
1935–39 D

3rd Row   280D DELIVERY VAN 'BISTO' 1937–39 E* ● 28K DELIVERY VAN 'MARSH'S SAUSAGES' 1935–39 D ● 28T DELIVERY VAN 'OVALTINE' 1936–39 D
(most of the 2nd type vans above show some signs of fatigue)

PRE-WAR AND EARLY POSTWAR DINKY COMMERCIALS

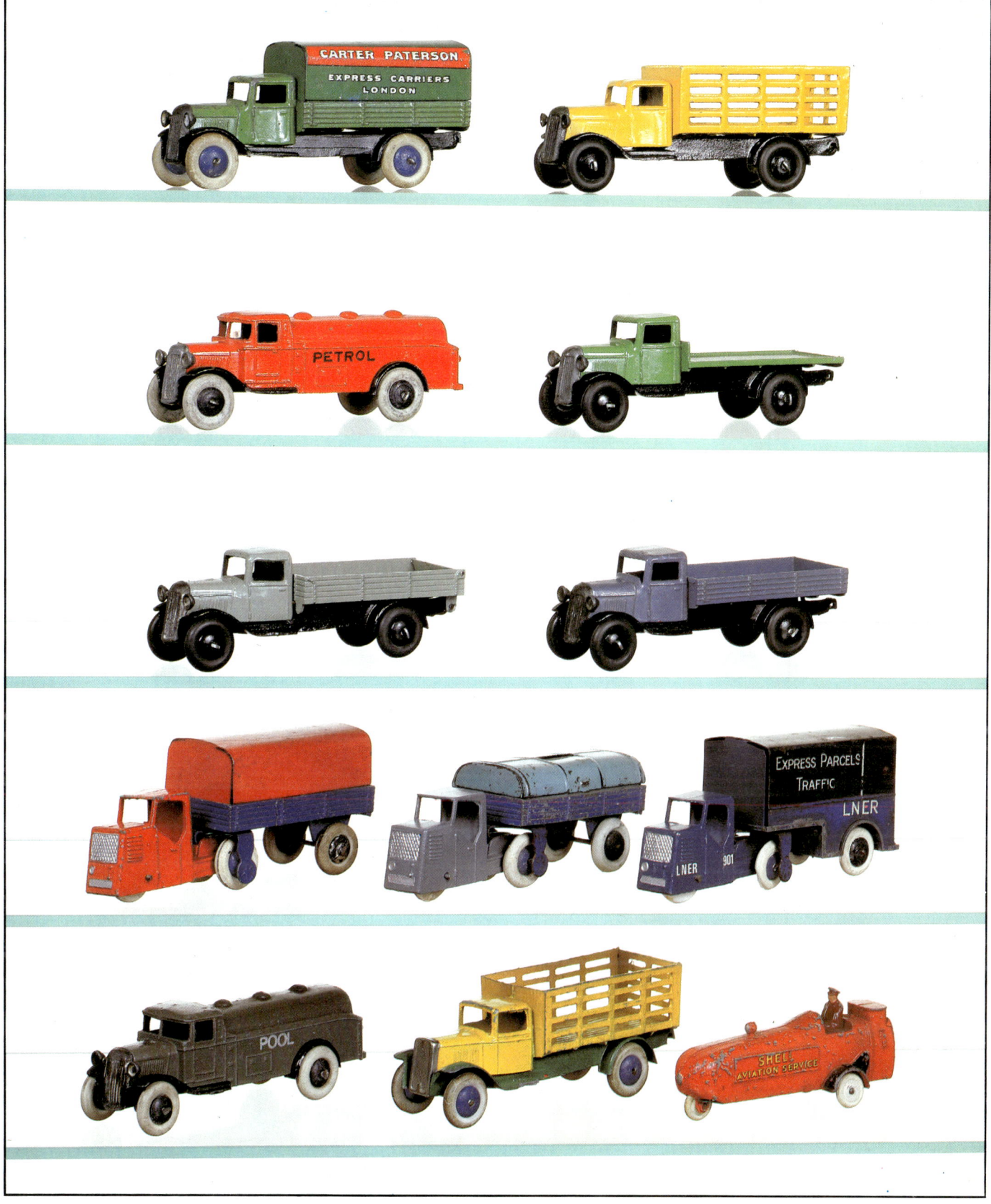

Top Row 25B COVERED WAGON 'CARTER PATERSON' 1935–41 D ● 25F MARKET GARDENER'S WAGON 1935–48 B
2nd Row 25D PETROL TANK WAGON 1946–47 B ● 25C FLAT TRUCK 1935–48 B
3rd Row 25E TIPPING WAGON 1946–48 B ● 25A OPEN WAGON 1946–48 B
4th Row 33A MECHANICAL HORSE 1935–40 B WITH 33C OPEN WAGON 1935–40 A AND TILT FROM 25B ● 33A MECHANICAL HORSE 1935–40 B WITH 33E DUST CART 1935–40 B ● 33R MECHANICAL HORSE AND BOX VAN TRAILER 'LNER' 1935–40 D TO E
5th Row 25D PETROL TANK WAGON 'POOL' 1946 D ● 25F MARKET GARDENER'S WAGON 1934–35 C (this has the early tin-plate grille) ● 60Y THOMPSON AIRFIELD REFUELLER 1938–41 D

Top Row 25B COVERED WAGON 1946–48 B (unusual colour) ● 25B COVERED WAGON 1946–48 B ● 25B COVERED WAGON 'CARTER PATERSON' 1946 D
2nd Row 25B COVERED WAGON 1948–50 B (this has the 3rd chassis with front bumper) ● 25G TRAILER 1946–50 A (with tin-plate rear hook 1950–63)
3rd Row 25D PETROL TANK WAGON 1948–50 B ● 25D PETROL TANK WAGON 'POOL' 1946 D ● 25D PETROL TANK WAGON 1946–48 B
4th Row 280 DELIVERY VAN 1948–51 A (a plain version of the 3rd type 28 Series van) ● 34C/492 LOUDSPEAKER VAN 1948–57 A (492 with box B)
5th Row 25C FLAT TRUCK 1946–48 A ● 25T FLAT TRUCK 1948–50 A ● 25T FLAT TRUCK 1948–50 A (only supplied with trailer in this period)

DINKY TOY VANS FROM THE 1950'S

Top Row 31A/450 TROJAN VAN 'ESSO' 1951–57 C ● 454 TROJAN VAN 'CYDRAX' 1957–59 C ● 455 TROJAN VAN 'BROOKE BOND' 1957–60 C
2nd Row 31D/453 TROJAN VAN 'OXO' 1953–54 D ● 31B/451 TROJAN VAN 'DUNLOP' 1952–57 C ● 31C/452 TROJAN VAN 'CHIVERS' 1953–57 C
3rd Row 480 BEDFORD CA VAN 'KODAK' 1954–56 C ● 481 BEDFORD CA VAN 'OVALTINE' 1955–60 C ● 482 BEDFORD CA VAN 'DINKY TOYS' 1956–60 C
4th Row 470 AUSTIN A40 VAN 'SHELL-BP' 1954–56 C ● 472 AUSTIN A40 VAN 'RALEIGH' 1957–60 C ● 471 AUSTIN A40 VAN 'NESTLÉS' 1955–63 C
5th Row 465 MORRIS COMMERCIAL VAN 'CAPSTAN' 1957–59 C ● 261 MORRIS Z VAN 'POST OFFICE TELEPHONES' 1956–61 C ● 260 MORRIS COMMERCIAL VAN 'ROYAL MAIL' 1955–61 C

SMALL DINKY COMMERCIALS FROM THE 1940'S AND 1950'S

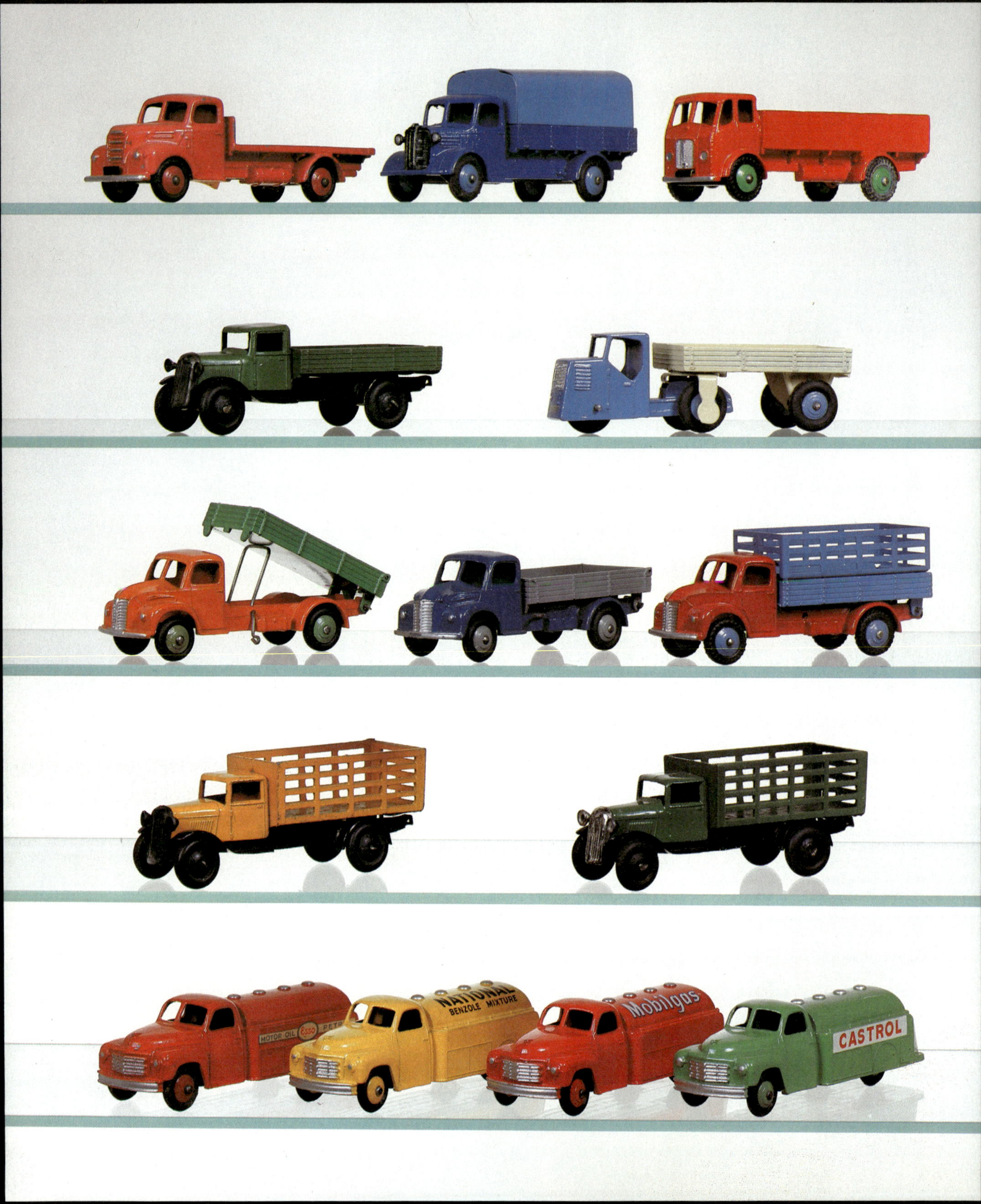

Top Row 30R/422 FORDSON THAMES FLAT TRUCK 1951–60 A ● 30S/413 AUSTIN COVERED WAGON 1950–60 B ● 25R/420 LEYLAND FORWARD CONTROL LORRY 1948–61 A

2nd Row 25A OPEN WAGON 1946–48 A ● 33W/415 MECHANICAL HORSE AND OPEN WAGON 1947–57 A (415 with box B)

3rd Row 30M/414 DODGE REAR TIPPING WAGON 1950–64 A ● 30M/414 DODGE REAR TIPPING WAGON 1950–64 A ● 30N/343 DODGE FARM PRODUCE WAGON 1950–64 A

4th Row 25F MARKET GARDENER'S WAGON 1946–48 B ● 25F MARKET GARDENER'S WAGON 1946–48 B

5th Row 30PB/442 STUDEBAKER TANKER 'ESSO' 1952–58 B ● 443 STUDEBAKER TANKER 'NATIONAL BENZOLE' 1957–59 B ● 30P/440 STUDEBAKER TANKER 'MOBILGAS' 1952–59 B ● 30PA/441 STUDEBAKER TANKER 'CASTROL' 1952–60 B

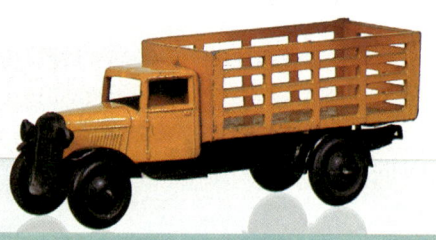

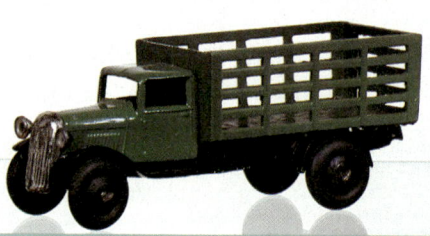

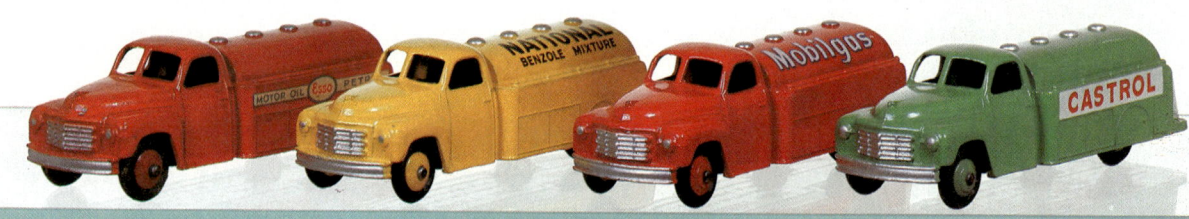

Top Row DINKY 25X COMMER BREAKDOWN LORRY 1940–54 A ● DINKY 25X COMMER BREAKDOWN LORRY 1950–54 A ● DINKY 430 COMMER BREAKDOWN LORRY 1954–63 A (this version with windows is post-1960)

2nd Row DINKY 30V/490 ELECTRIC DAIRY VAN 'EXPRESS DAIRIES' 1949–60 A ● DINKY 30V/491 ELECTRIC DAIRY VAN 'NCB' 1949–60 B (for export only from 1954)

3rd Row DINKY 27G/342 MOTO-CART 1949–61 A ● DINKY 30E BEDFORD BREAKDOWN TRUCK 1947–48 A (with black wings and open cab rear window 1935–46 B) ● DINKY 14A/400 BEV ELECTRIC TRUCK 1948–60 A

4th Row CORGI 455 KARRIER BANTAM 2-TONNER 1957–60 A (in red without windows, but with 'CWS Soft Drinks' transfers: Mettoy *ca* 1955 B) ● DINKY 27F/344 PLYMOUTH STATION WAGON 1950–60 B

5th Row DINKY 25M/410 BEDFORD END TIPPER 1948–63 A ● DINKY 25W/411 BEDFORD TRUCK 1949–60 B ● DINKY 25V/252 BEDFORD REFUSE WAGON 1948–64 B

CORGI SMALL COMMERCIALS FROM THE LATE 1950'S AND EARLY 1960'S

Top Row   465 COMMER ¾-TON PICK-UP 1963–65 A ● 420 FORD THAMES AIRBORNE CARAVAN 1961–67 A ● 441 VOLKSWAGEN VAN 'TOBLERONE' 1963–67 B

2nd Row   409 JEEP FC 150 1959–65 A (as 470 with suspension, interior and tilt 1965–72) ● 434 VOLKSWAGEN KOMBI 1963–66 A ● 466 COMMER ¾-TON MILK FLOAT 1964–65 A

3rd Row   428 KARRIER 'MISTER SOFTEE' ICE CREAM VAN 1963–66 A ● 474 FORD THAMES WALL'S ICE CREAM VAN 1965–67 A (this version has 'chimes', 447 does not)

4th Row   404 BEDFORD DORMOBILE 1956–60 A ● 403 BEDFORD CA VAN 'DAILY EXPRESS' 1956–60 B ● 403M BEDFORD CA VAN 'KLG PLUGS' 1956–59 B

5th Row   458 ERF 64G EARTH DUMPER 1958–67 A ● 454 COMMER 5-TON FLAT TRUCK 1957–62 A ● 452 COMMER 5-TON DROP-SIDE WAGON 1956–63 A with 1487 MILK CHURNS LOAD 1960–65 A

Top Row   502 FODEN FLAT TRUCK 1948–52 C (this is the 1st Foden cab) ● 503 FODEN FLAT TRUCK WITH TAILBOARD 1947–48 C (with hook 1948–52) ● 502 FODEN FLAT TRUCK 1947–48 C (with hook 1948–52)

2nd Row   504 FODEN 14-TON TANKER 1948–52 C ● 501 FODEN WAGON 1947–48 C (with hook 1948–52)

3rd Row   502/902 FODEN FLAT TRUCK 1952–60 C (this is the 2nd Foden cab) ● 502/902 FODEN FLAT TRUCK 1952–60 C (an unusual colour) ● 502/902 FODEN FLAT TRUCK 1952–60 C

4th Row   503/903 FODEN FLAT TRUCK WITH TAILBOARD 1952–60 C (an unusual colour) ● 503/903 FODEN FLAT TRUCK WITH TAILBOARD 1952–60 C

5th Row   501/901 FODEN WAGON 1952–57 C ● 505/905 FODEN FLAT TRUCK WITH CHAINS 1952–64 C

Top Row	514/917 GUY VAN 'SPRATT'S' 1953–56 E ● 514 GUY VAN 'LYON'S' *ca* 1951–52 E*
2nd Row	918 GUY VAN 'EVER READY' 1955–58 D ● 919 GUY VAN 'GOLDEN SHRED' 1957–58 E
3rd Row	514 GUY VAN 'SLUMBERLAND' *ca* 1949–51 D ● 514 GUY VAN 'WEETABIX' 1952–53 E*
4th Row	513/913/433 GUY FLAT TRUCK WITH TAILBOARD 1948–58 B ● 512 GUY FLAT TRUCK 1947–48 B ● 512/912 GUY FLAT TRUCK 1948–56 B
5th Row	511/911/431 GUY 4-TON LORRY 1948–58 B ● 912/432 GUY FLAT TRUCK 1954–58 B ● 513/913/433 GUY FLAT TRUCK WITH TAILBOARD 1948–58 B

DINKY TOY TRUCKS OF THE 1950'S AND EARLY 1960'S

Top Row 522/922/408 BEDFORD S LORRY 1952–63 B ● 522/922/408 BEDFORD S LORRY 1952–63 B ● 521/921/409 BEDFORD ARTICULATED LORRY 1948–63 B
2nd Row 532/932/418 LEYLAND COMET WAGON WITH HINGED TAILBOARD 1952–59 B ● 532/932/418 LEYLAND COMET WAGON WITH HINGED TAILBOARD 1952–59 B ● 533/933/419 LEYLAND COMET CEMENT WAGON 1953–59 C
3rd Row 531/931/417 LEYLAND COMET LORRY 1949–59 B ● 531/931/417 LEYLAND COMET LORRY 1949–59 B ● 531/931/417 LEYLAND COMET LORRY 1949–59 B
4th Row 431 GUY WARRIOR 4-TON LORRY 1958–64 D ● 432 GUY WARRIOR FLAT TRUCK 1958–64 D
5th Row 958 GUY WARRIOR SNOW PLOUGH 1961–65 C

Top Row 977 SERVICING PLATFORM VEHICLE 1960–64 C ● 936 LEYLAND 8-WHEELED CHASSIS 1964–69 B
2nd Row 504 FODEN 14-TON TANKER 1952–53 D (unusual colour for the 2nd cab) ● 504/941 FODEN TANKER 'MOBILGAS' 1953–56 D
3rd Row 504 FODEN 14-TON TANKER 1952–53 C ● 943 LEYLAND OCTOPUS TANKER 'ESSO' 1958–64 D
4th Row 942 FODEN TANKER 'REGENT' 1955–57 D ● 944 LEYLAND OCTOPUS TANKER 'SHELL-BP' 1963–70 C
5th Row 935 LEYLAND OCTOPUS FLAT TRUCK WITH CHAINS 1964–66 E ● 934 LEYLAND OCTOPUS WAGON 1956–64 C

Top Row 425 BEDFORD TK COAL LORRY 1964–69 B ● 435 BEDFORD TK TIPPER 1964–71 A
2nd Row 960 ALBION LORRY-MOUNTED CONCRETE MIXER 1960–69 B ● 959 FODEN DUMP TRUCK 1961–69 B
3rd Row 966 LEYLAND MARREL MULTI-BUCKET UNIT 1961–64 B ● 434 BEDFORD TK CRASH TRUCK 1964–66 B (in red and white 1966–73 A)
4th Row 965 EUCLID DUMP TRUCK 1955–69 A ● 930 BEDFORD PALLET-JEKTA VAN 'DINKY TOYS' 1960–64 C

DINKY TOY TELEVISION VEHICLES

Top Row   969 BBC TV EXTENDING MAST VEHICLE 1959–64 C
2nd Row   967 BBC TV MOBILE CONTROL ROOM 1959–64 B ● 968 BBC TV ROVING EYE VEHICLE 1959–64 B
3rd Row   987 ABC TV CONTROL ROOM 1962–70 B ● 988 ABC TV TRANSMITTER VAN 1962–69 B

Top Row   **DINKY TOYS 990 CAR TRANSPORTER AND 4 CARS 1956–58 D CONTAINING:** 582/982 BEDFORD PULLMORE CAR TRANSPORTER 1953–64 B ●
154 HILLMAN MINX 1956–58 B ● 156 ROVER 75 1956–60 B ● 161 AUSTIN SOMERSET 1956–60 B ● 162 FORD ZEPHYR 1956–60 B

2nd Row   **CORGI TOYS GIFT SET 16 1961–66 C CONTAINING:** 1126 ECURIE ECOSSE RACING CAR TRANSPORTER 1961–66 B ● 150S VANWALL RACING CAR
1961–65 A (as 150 without suspension and driver 1957–61) ● 151A LOTUS MARK XI LE MANS 1961–64 B (as 151 without driver 1958–61, this model is inside the
transporter!) ● 152S BRM RACING CAR 1961–65 A (as 152 without driver and suspension 1958–61)

3rd Row   **CORGI TOYS GIFT SET 1 ca 1961 C (different contents 1957–62) CONTAINING:** 1101 BEDFORD CARRIMORE CAR TRANSPORTER 1957–62 A ●
305 TRIUMPH TR3 1960–64 B ● 216 AUSTIN A40 1959–62 B ● 226 MORRIS MINI-MINOR 1960–71 A ● 234 FORD CONSUL CLASSIC 1961–65 A

Top Row   **985 DINKY CAR CARRIER AND TRAILER 1958–63 C COMPRISING:** 984 LEYLAND CAR CARRIER 1958–63 C ● 985 TRAILER FOR CAR CARRIER 1958–63 B

2nd Row   DINKY 974 AEC HOYNOR CAR TRANSPORTER 1968–75 B

3rd Row   **CORGI TOYS GIFT SET 48 1969 C CONTAINING:** 1148 SCAMMELL HIGHWAYMAN CARRIMORE CAR TRANSPORTER 1969 B ● 345 MGC GT 1968–69 A ● 340 SUNBEAM IMP MONTE CARLO RALLY 1967–69 A ● 258 THE SAINT'S VOLVO P1800 1965–69 A ● 249 MORRIS MINI-COOPER WITH WICKERWORK 1965–68 A ● 339 MINI-COOPER 'S' MONTE CARLO RALLY 1967–72 A ● 226 MORRIS MINI-MINOR 1960–71 A

Top Row 110/2 AEC MAMMOTH MAJOR 8 FLAT TRUCK 1960–62 D ● CB106 FOUR WHEEL TRAILER 1961–62 B
2nd Row 110/28 AEC MAMMOTH MAJOR 8 'LONDON BRICK CO' 1960–63 C ● 109/2P ERF 68G FLAT TRUCK WITH PLANKS 1960–63 C
3rd Row 110/3 AEC MAMMOTH MAJOR 8 'BRITISH ROAD SERVICES' 1959–63 C ● 158A/2 BEDFORD 10-TON ARTICULATED TANKER 'SHELL BP' 1961–63 E
4th Row 106A/OC AUSTIN 503 ARTICULATED FLAT TRUCK WITH MGA IN CRATE 1960–63 D ● 110/4 AEC MAMMOTH MAJOR 8 TANKER 'SHELL BP' 1961–63 E
5th Row 109/3B ERF 68G WAGON WITH BARRELS 1960–63 E ● 111A/1 FORD THAMES TRADER 'BRITISH RAILWAYS' 1959–63 C

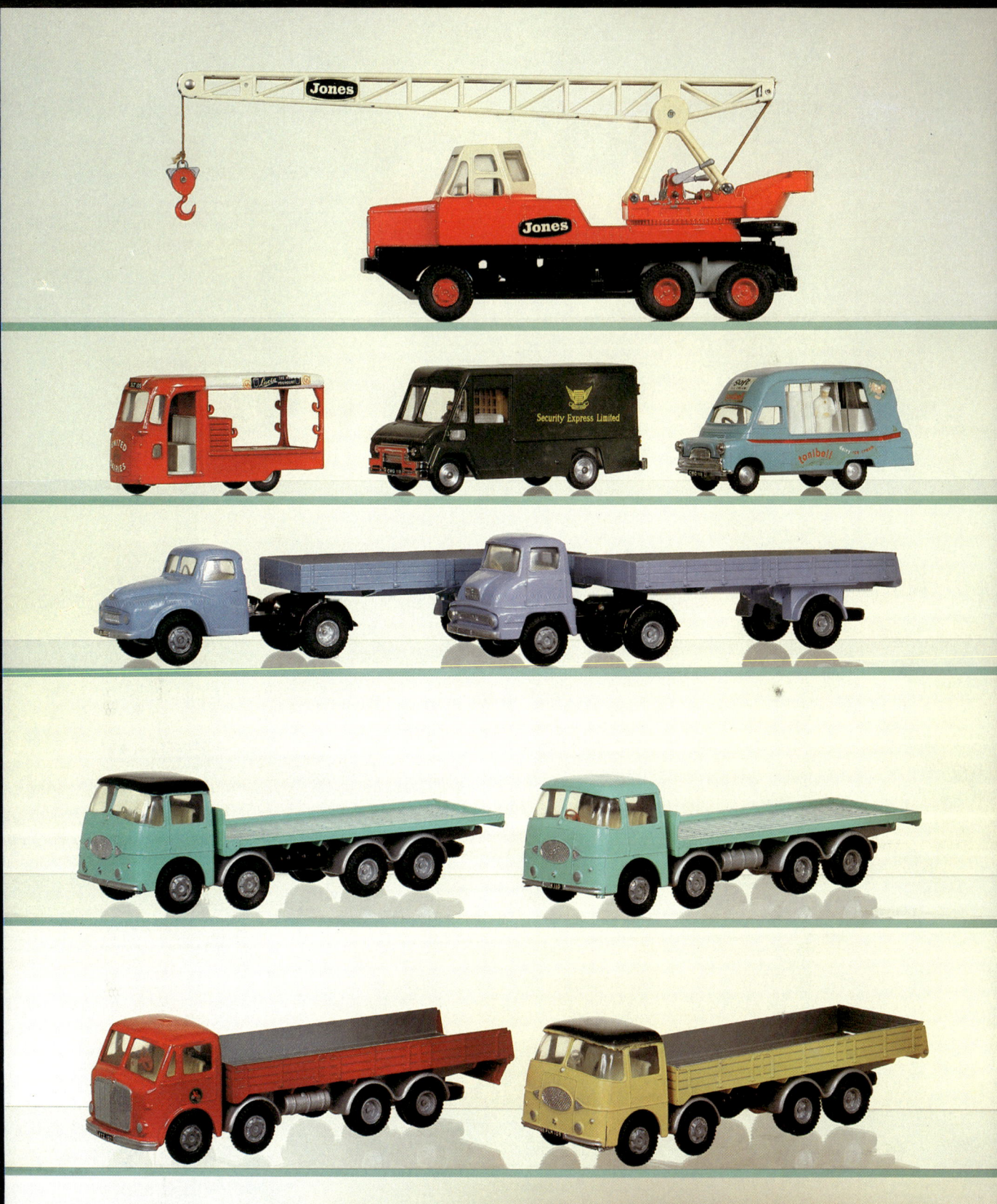

Top Row 117 JONES KL 10/10 MOBILE CRANE 1961–63 C
2nd Row 122 UNITED DAIRIES MILK FLOAT 1961–66 B ● 273 COMMER SECURITY VAN (money box) 1965–67 C ● 265 BEDFORD CA TONIBELL ICE CREAM VAN 1964–67 B
3rd Row 106A/1 AUSTIN 503 ARTICULATED TRUCK 1959–63 C ●111A/1 FORD THAMES TRADER ARTICULATED TRUCK 1961–62 C
4th Row 109/2 ERF 68G FLAT TRUCK 1960–62 C ● 109/2 ERF 68G FLAT TRUCK 1960–62 C
5th Row 110/3 AEC MAMMOTH MAJOR 8 'BRITISH ROAD SERVICES' 1959–63 C ● 109/3 ERF 68G OPEN WAGON 1960–63 C

SMALL-SCALE COMMERCIALS

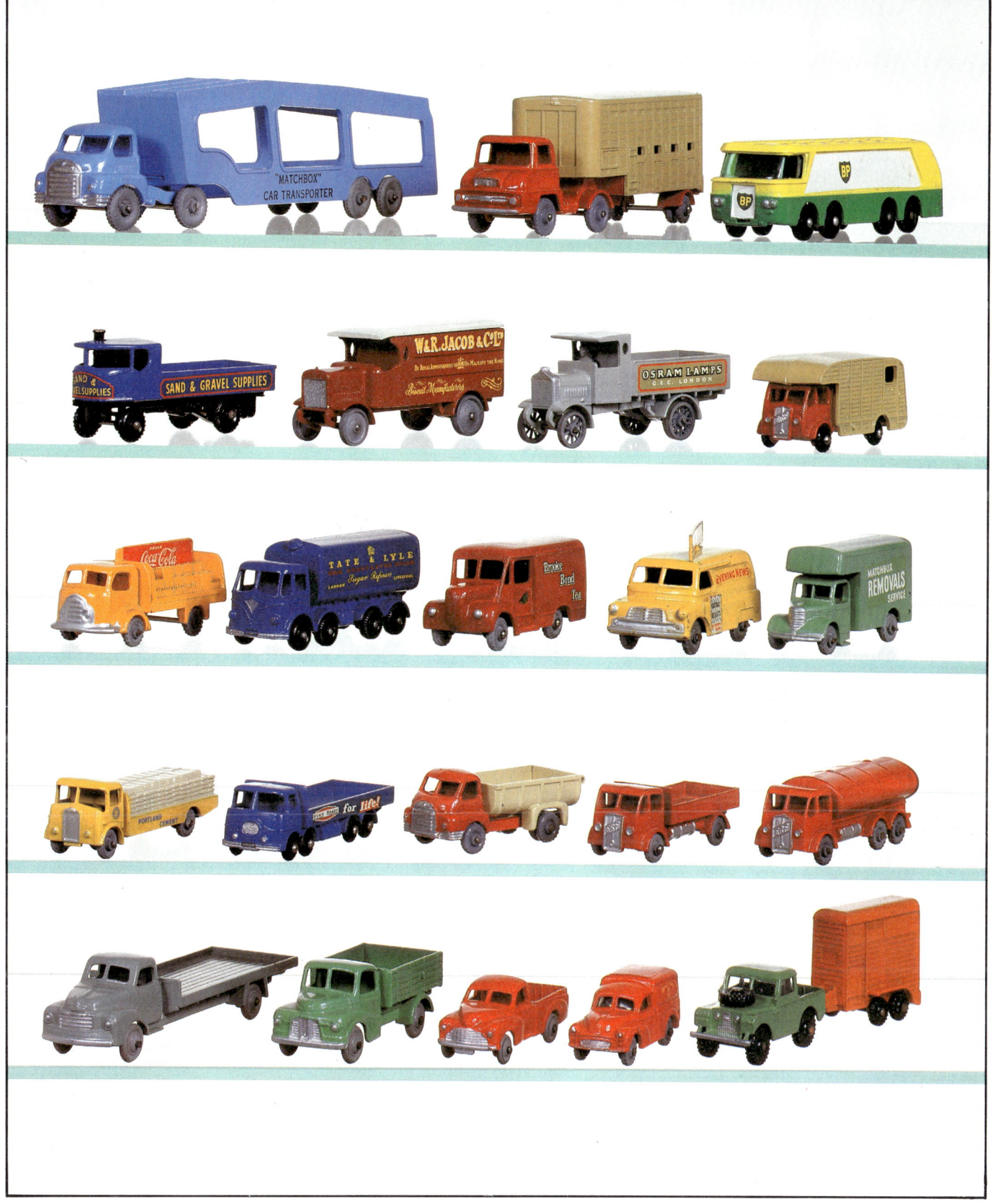

Top Row MATCHBOX ACCESSORY PACK A2 BEDFORD CAR TRANSPORTER 1958–63 A ● MATCHBOX MAJOR PACK M7 FORD THAMES TRADER CATTLE TRUCK 1960–63 A ● MATCHBOX MAJOR PACK M1 'BP' TANKER 1961–65 A

2nd Row MATCHBOX MODELS OF YESTERYEAR Y4 1918 SENTINEL STEAM WAGON 1956–60 C ● MATCHBOX MODELS OF YESTERYEAR Y7 LEYLAND 4-TON VAN 'JACOB' 1957–61 C ● MATCHBOX MODELS OF YESTERYEAR Y6 1916 AEC 'Y'-TYPE LORRY 'OSRAM LAMPS' 1958–61 C ● MATCHBOX 35 ERF MARSHALL HORSE BOX 1957–64 A

3rd Row MATCHBOX 37 KARRIER BANTAM 2-TON 'COCA-COLA' 1957–58 A (the 1st of 3 similar models 1957–66) ● MATCHBOX 10 FODEN 15-TON SUGAR CONTAINER 'TATE AND LYLE' 1960–66 A ● MATCHBOX 47 TROJAN 1-TON 'BROOKE BOND TEA' 1958–63 A ● MATCHBOX 42 BEDFORD CA 'EVENING NEWS' VAN 1957–65 A ● MATCHBOX 17 BEDFORD 'MATCHBOX REMOVALS' VAN 1958–60 A (the 2nd of 2 similar models 1955–60)

4th Row MATCHBOX 51 ALBION CHIEFTAIN LORRY 'PORTLAND CEMENT' 1958–64 A ● MATCHBOX 20 ERF 68G 'EVER READY' 1959–65 A ● MATCHBOX 40 BEDFORD 'S' 7-TON TIPPER 1957–61 A ● MATCHBOX 20 ERF LORRY 1956–59 A ● MATCHBOX 11 ERF PETROL TANKER 'ESSO' 1958–64 A (the 2nd of 2 similar models)

5th Row DUBLO-DINKY 066 BEDFORD FLAT TRUCK 1957–60 A ● DUBLO-DINKY 064 AUSTIN LORRY 1957–62 A ● DUBLO-DINKY 065 MORRIS OXFORD PICK-UP 1957–60 A ● DUBLO-DINKY 068 MORRIS MINOR ROYAL MAIL VAN 1959–64 B ● DUBLO-DINKY 073 LAND ROVER WITH HORSE BOX AND HORSE 1960–64 A

From Noddy to James Bond
Character toys

Toys of popular characters first appeared with the success of the cinema in the 1920's, and were a logical extension of the 'novelty' genre of tinplate toys from Germany and the USA . Being more geared towards the manufacture of real vehicles, the die-cast toy producers were slower to respond. Tootsietoy made two unsuccessful entries into this field in the 1930's: the Funnies set, based on popular comic-strip characters, and the Buck Rogers Rocket Ship set, which were the world's first die-cast space toys. At this point it should be said that it is difficult to categorise character toys by vehicular subject, since many of the 'cars' mentioned here can also fly, float, submerge or travel through space.

The majority of English-made character toys of the pre- and immediate post-war years were figures, such as the Britains Snow White and the Seven Dwarfs set and the Mickey Mouse series by Charbens. This latter included an item called Mickey's Fire Engine, which could have claimed to be the first English die-cast character vehicle had the fire engine itself been based on a 'character'. As it was not, this distinction goes to the four-inch and two-inch Noddy Cars made by Morestone and Budgie in a series of Noddy items from the late 1950's and early 1960's. The Budgie Toy Supercar of 1962 was the first die-cast space vehicle to be made here, and was a model of a model, since it was based on the 'star' of a Gerry Anderson TV puppet series.

Gerry Anderson designs were used for most of the Dinky character toys, the first of which was Lady Penelope's car from the 'Thunderbirds' series, a pink six-wheeled rocket-firing Rolls Royce with the very '60's number 'FAB 1'. Another piece of period kitsch appeared the previous year (1965), a pink-and-green veteran Morris Oxford festooned with slogans like 'Gear' and 'Way Out' and containing a group called the 'Dinky Beats'. Despite being made in Liverpool, it does not represent any particular group, since this one has only *three* members. The Gerry Anderson vehicles included the only mechanised Dinky Toys, key-less clockwork motors being fitted to Sam's Car (1969) and Ed Straker's Car (1971). The Pink Panther Car introduced in 1972 (*another* pink car!) was powered by a heavy flywheel set in motion by a pull-through rack rod: this mechanism was first used by a French tinplate manufacturer almost 100 years before, one of the subjects, coincidentally, being a cat.

Although the Gerry Anderson vehicles were the most action-packed of all Dinky Toys, they were generally rather clumsy compared to the Corgi character toys of the 1960's. The first of these, possibly the most famous toy of the 1960's, was James Bond's Aston Martin DB5 from the film 'Goldfinger'. Although it had the shortest production span of the four Corgi models of this car, the original 1965 issue is much the most common today, a testament to its enormous popularity despite the fact that it was incorrectly finished in gold rather than silver. It had many 'actions', yet these features hardly disturbed the smooth lines of the car, and the toy won several design awards. It was replaced in 1968 by a slightly larger version with even more operating features but the plastic bumpers made it more fragile and it is now more difficult to find in good condition. A simpler $^1/_{36}$th scale model replaced it in 1978. This is still current, as is the small Corgi Juniors version introduced in 1968. Following this successful debut in the field, Corgi produced a large number of character toys, and the pattern has continued to this day. Some have been little more than re-vamps of already existing castings but most have been accurately based on vehicles from comic strips, films or television series.

The excellent model of Chitty-Chitty-Bang-Bang which appeared in 1968 owed much to the Corgi Classics range, while the short-lived and fragile Popeye's Paddle Wagon, which is marginally more of a car than a boat, is the most valuable Corgi Toy today. Increased tooling costs have meant that more recent character toys have fewer gimmicks than their predecessors. The success of a character toy depends very heavily on the success of the character, and it is likely that many of the heroes or villains portrayed in today's toys will be unknown in the future, just as Corgi's once-popular Monkeemobile is no longer considered desirable.

Top Row   805 THE HARDY BOYS' 1912 ROLLS ROYCE 1970 B ● 266 CHITTY CHITTY BANG BANG 1968–72 C
2nd Row   801 NODDY'S CAR WITH NODDY BIG EARS AND GOLLIWOG 1969–71 B ● 804 NODDY AND HIS CAR 1970–77 B ● 801 NODDY'S CAR WITH NODDY BIG EARS AND TUBBY 1970 C
3rd Row   808 BASIL BRUSH'S CAR (1910 Renault) 1972–73 A ● 807 MAGIC ROUNDABOUT CAR (Citroën) 1971–74 A ● 859 MR McHENRY'S TRIKE 1972–74 A
4th Row   267 BATMOBILE 1966-current A (this has the earlier wheels) ● 336 JAMES BOND'S TOYOTA 2000 1968–69 A ● 270 JAMES BOND'S ASTON MARTIN DB5 1968–77 A (the 2nd of 3 similar models)
5th Row   9004 WORLD OF WOOSTER 1927 BENTLEY 1967–69 B ● 497 THE MAN FROM UNCLE CAR (Oldsmobile) 1966–69 A ● **GIFT SET 40 THE AVENGERS 1967–69**
C CONTAINING: JOHN STEED's 1927 BENTLEY AND EMMA PEEL'S LOTUS ELAN

Made for display
Collectors' series

Although primarily intended for older and more discerning children, the Matchbox Models of Yesteryear were undoubtedly the first toys to have a substantial adult following in their own time. As a result they are easier to find in good condition than other toys of the same age. This appreciation was well deserved, for in the late 1950's they were the most detailed die-cast models in the world. What is now termed the 1st Series of Models of Yesteryear encompassed the whole spectrum of land-based transport in the early 20th century – from locomotives and traction engines to lorries and cars and can be distinguished from later models by the absence of plastic parts, except for the tyres of the three cars. The last model in this style, and the most desirable today, was a Shand-Mason Horse-drawn Fire Engine introduced in 1960. Successive models, the first of which appeared in the same year, have been almost exclusively of cars, with plastic being used for the seats, and for hoods and other details from the mid-1960's. The castings are generally less complicated than for the first series, and more common parts are used to reduce production costs. As a result, Yesteryears have become to some extent less successful as *models*, and the rather garish colour schemes used in the 1970's did not help in this respect.

Over the years, some of the same developments occurred with Yesteryears as with other toy ranges, for example a high proportion of the new releases of the late 1960's were of American subjects and there has been a general increase in size and scale. The most important recent development has been the introduction of vans with different period advertising, a theme which was already popular among collectors of old toys. While this undoubtedly helps in reducing tooling costs, it is unfortunate that the price for a Yesteryear model has risen from about twice that of a regular Matchbox model in 1956 to over four times today, making the series much less competitive with the superior collectors' models from France and Italy.

The construction detail which sets the Corgi Classics range apart from such competitiors as Solido from France and Rio from Italy, both of which started to produce collector's models at about the same time as Corgi and are still in production, was the use of individual stub axles for each wheel, an important feature bearing in mind the exposed suspension of early cars. It is unfortunate that these excellent models had such a short production life, for they would have been much more successful given today's vastly expanded collectors' market.

The demise of Corgi Classics, the increasingly toy-like quality of the Models of Yesteryear and the growing number of adult collectors all contributed to the foundation of the white-metal industry in the late 1960's. These were the first models to be produced exclusively for adult collectors, and as such have nothing in common with models primarily intended as toys, except in terms of scale. White metal is a very soft alloy and since no compromise has to be made between detail and robustness, the models are generally far too fragile to be played with. Two parallel ranges of subject were chosen; buses to $1/76$th scale, Pirate Models being the most successful in this field; and sports and racing cars to $1/43$rd scale, John Day and Paddy Stanley being the first exponents. These models were only available in kit form, and considerable skill was required in assembly as the quality of casting was rather variable. As casting techniques improved, models of larger cars appeared, particularly in the range made by Western Models, founded in 1974 and the most successful manufacturer to date. Western was the first white-metal producer to supply the models in fully-finished as well as in kit form. Most ranges are now available in either form. The range of subjects has also expanded considerably in the last ten years. There is still a predominance of sports and racing cars and 1930's exotica, but there are also models of popular saloon cars which were omitted from the toy ranges of the 1950's and 1960's, for example the Ford E93A Popular, Jaguar Mark VII, Morris 1000 Traveller and other latter-day classics.

CORGI CLASSICS

Top Row 900/9002 1927 BENTLEY 3-LITRE 1964–69 B ● 900/9001 1927 BENTLEY 3-LITRE LE MANS CAR 1964–69 B ● 9013 FORD MODEL 'T' WITH RAISED HOOD 1965–69 B (supplied with man in cranking position)
2nd Row 90031 1910 RENAULT 12/16 COUPE 1965–69 B ● 9032 1910 RENAULT 12/16 COUPE 1965–69 B ● 901/9011 1915 FORD MODEL 'T' 1964–69 B (supplied with driver and passenger)
3rd Row 9021 1910 DAIMLER 38-HP TOURER 1965–69 B ● JOHN STEED'S BENTLEY FROM GIFT SET 40 THE AVENGERS 1967–69 C

BOXED SETS

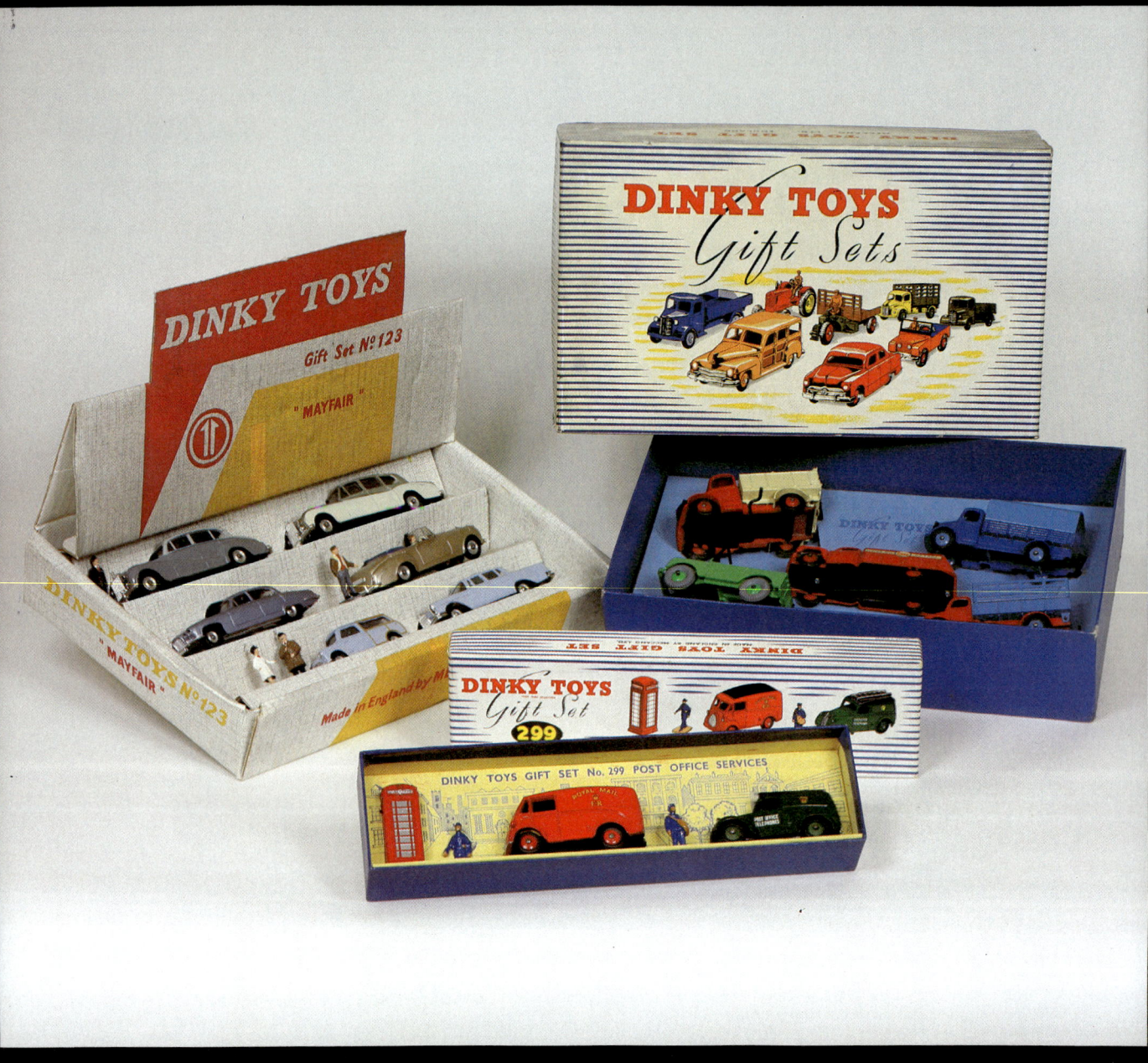

Left **DINKY TOYS GIFT SET 123 MAYFAIR 1963–64 D CONTAINING:** 150 ROLLS ROYCE SILVER WRAITH 1959–64 B ● 198 ROLLS ROYCE PHANTOM V 1962–69 B ● 142 JAGUAR MARK X 1962–69 A ● 194 BENTLEY 'S' SERIES COUPE 1961–67 B ● 199 AUSTIN SEVEN COUNTRYMAN 1961–70 A ● 186 MERCEDES-BENZ 220SE 1961–67 A

Right **DINKY TOYS GIFT SET 2 COMMERCIAL VEHICLES 1952–53 D CONTAINING:** 25M/410 BEDFORD END TIPPER 1948–63 A ● 30S/413 AUSTIN COVERED WAGON 1950–60 B ● 30PB/442 STUDEBAKER TANKER 'ESSO' 1952–58 B ● 27D/340 LAND ROVER 1950–70 A ● 30N/343 DODGE FARM PRODUCE WAGON 1950–64 A

Bottom **DINKY TOYS GIFT SET 299 POST OFFICE SERVICES 1958 D CONTAINING:** 12C/750 TELEPHONE BOX 1936–62 A (pre-war version has black window frames) ● 12D/011 TELEGRAPH MESSENGER 1938–60 A (pre-war version is in darker blue) ● 260 MORRIS COMMERCIAL ROYAL MAIL VAN 1955–61 C ● 12E/012 POSTMAN 1938–60 A (pre-war version is in darker blue) ● 261 MORRIS 'Z' POST OFFICE TELEPHONES VAN 1956–61 C

BROOKLIN MODELS (white metal fully-built)

Top Row 3 1930 FORD MODEL A VICTORIA ● 5 1930 FORD MODEL A COUPE ● 4 1937 CHEVROLET COUPE
2nd Row 1 1933 PIERCE ARROW SILVER ARROW ● 2 1948 TUCKER TORPEDO ● 6 1932 PACKARD LIGHT 8
3rd Row 7 1934 CHRYSLER AIRFLOW ● 12 1931 HUDSON BOAT-TAIL ROADSTER ● 9 1940 FORD SEDAN DELIVERY 'FORD'
4th Row 11 1956 LINCOLN CONTINENTAL II ● 15 1949 MERCURY 2-DOOR SEDAN ● 10 1949 BUICK ROADMASTER
5th Row 14 1940 CADILLAC V16 ● 8A CHRYSLER NEWPORT 1940 INDIANAPOLIS PACEMAKER ● 13 1956 FORD THUNDERBIRD

WHITE METAL MODELS

Top Row   K & R REPLICAS KITS ● K & R 4 1953–55 TRIUMPH TR 2 ● K & R 5 1957 TRIUMPH TR 3 ● K & R 1 1967 AUSTIN HEALEY 3000 MK III

2nd Row   WILLS FINECAST KITS ● WF 407 1928 AUSTIN 7 SALOON ● WF 409 1924 MORRIS BULLNOSE ● WF 403 1935 RILEY IMP ● WF 410 FRASER-NASH TT REPLICA

3rd Row   WF 405 1934 AUSTIN ULSTER 2-SEATER ● WF 401 1922 CITROËN 5CV CLOVERLEAF ● WF 404 1928 AUSTIN 7 TOURER ● WF 406 1934 MORGAN 3-WHEELER

4th Row   ABINGDON CLASSICS KITS ● AB 401 MG HIGH SPEED SERVICE VAN ● AB 101 1946 MG TC MIDGET ● JEM 1 1931 MG C TYPE MONTLHERY MIDGET ● JEM 9 1930 MG M TYPE MIDGET

5th Row   MOTOR KITS ● FORD Y VAN 'ATCO' ● WOLSELEY WASP ● PEUGEOT ANDREAU

WESTERN MODELS (white metal fully-built or kits)

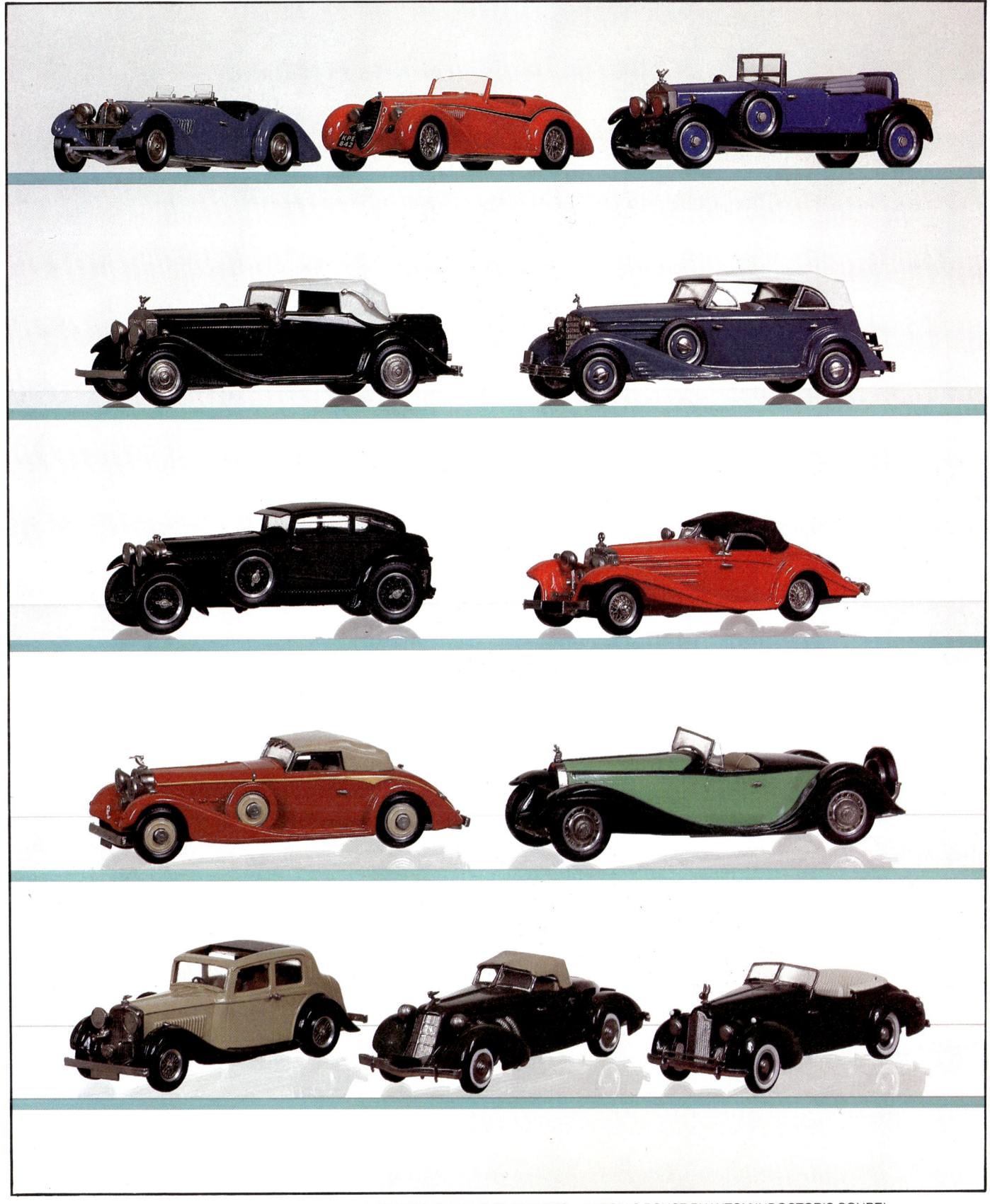

Top Row   39 1938 BUGATTI TYPE 57 CORSICA ● 33 1938 ALFA ROMEO 2900/B CS TOURING ● 27 ROLLS ROYCE PHANTOM II 'DOCTOR'S COUPE'
2nd Row   8 1933 ROLLS ROYCE PHANTOM II ● 28 CADILLAC DUAL PHAETON
3rd Row   32 BENTLEY 6½ LITRE BERNATO ● 1 1938 MERCEDES-BENZ 540K ROADSTER
4th Row   20 1933 HISPANO-SUIZA 68 ● 29 1932 BUGATTI TYPE 41 LA ROYALE ROADSTER ESDERS
5th Row   34 1936 BENTLEY MULLINER SALOON ● 5 1935 AUBURN 851 SPEEDSTER ● 31 PACKARD DARRIN

WESTERN MODELS (white metal fully-built or kits)

Top Row   WMS 38 MG EX 135 GARDNER RECORD CAR ● WMS 19 MERCEDES-BENZ C111/3 RECORD CAR
2nd Row   WMS 23 1927 SUNBEAM 1000HP RECORD CAR
3rd Row   WMS 9 MALCOLM CAMPBELL'S 1933 BLUEBIRD II ● WMS 15 1929 GOLDEN ARROW RECORD CAR
4th Row   WMS 25 JOHN COBB'S 1939 NAPIER-RAILTON RECORD CAR
5th Row   WMS 30 GEORGE EYSTON'S 1937 THUNDERBOLT RECORD CAR

Past and present
Building a collection

Identification

The overwhelming majority of models are marked with the manufacturer's name and country of origin. Most post-war issues are also marked with the name of the vehicle and sometimes the catalogue number. Books are available on each of the major manufacturers which give details on dimensions, production dates and the range of colours for each model. It should be said that none of these sources would claim to be totally complete, particularly in regard to colours, and that the omission of a particular variation does not necessarily imply that it is a rare or valuable one. Rather it is the case that the variations included are those known to the authors at the time of writing and can in most cases safely be assumed to exist. Information on the lesser-known manufacturers is more difficult to obtain, but articles on these appear from time to time in the collectors' journals.

Perhaps the most important indication of value is the differentiation between pre-war Dinky Toys and their post-war re-issues. In this respect the sources which have appeared to date have not been too helpful, and there are as many exceptions as adherents to any 'rules' concerning wheels and tyres. The only fail-safe check is the thickness of the axles and the bore of the axle-retaining holes in the body of the vehicle: pre-war axles have a diameter of .062 of an inch (1.58mm) in holes of .070 of an inch in diameter, while the post-war equivalents are .078 of an inch (1.98mm) and .088 of an inch, respectively. This change can be dated from Meccano drawings of August 1945, some months before the first re-issues appeared. It is not necessary to carry a micrometer; the difference is discernible to the naked eye when two examples are compared.

Recognition of original paint cannot be so easily quantified and only comes with experience. There are a few simple checks as to whether a model has been re-painted or not. Most good repaints have involved dismantling the model and it should be possible to tell if the axle ends or rivets have been disturbed.

Some complete copies of early Dinky Toys have been produced recently. Fortunately it is not yet economic to produce copies in pressure die-cast mazak, so most copies are made of white metal and can be recognised by weight. In any case, most copies are clearly identified as such. A greater problem is caused by some of the copies of lead-alloy Dinky Toys, where the weight is almost identical and in some cases the original marking is left intact. However, the prices of the real Dinkies should be sufficient to deter the novice collector until he or she has enough experience to recognise the copies by feel.

Another pit-fall in identification can be caused by cleverly-done 'chops' where, for example, post-war Dinky bodies can be made to fit pre-war chassis and artificially 'shabbied' to look original. Again, there may be no way of identifying these fakes and much depends on the integrity of the 'chopper'. 'Chopping' can also be performed on some of the larger Dinky Toy commercial vehicles such as the Guy or Foden lorries, resulting in 'rare' colour combinations.

Evaluation

The highest value for any model is for an example in mint (as new) condition with the original box. Individual boxes were made for larger Dinky Toys until 1954, and for all Dinky Toys after that date. All Lesney, Corgi and Spot-On models were issued with boxes. It should be said that the presence of a box greatly affecting the value of a toy is a peculiarly British feature, and does not apply to the same extent elsewhere. It should also be stressed that the empty box has no great value in itself.

In general, the extent to which the value is determined by condition depends on the availability of the model in *any* condition. For example, because of the difficulty in finding fatigue-free pre-war Dinky Toys, an example with good metal but no paint can be more valuable than one with good paint but crumbling metal, while on the other hand a 1960's mint-and-boxed Yesteryear model can be worth up to three times as much as the same example without the box, since the basic model is easy to find in good condition. In the same way, the value increment for a rare colour or livery depends on the availability of the 'common' one. For example, a rare livery on a first-type 28 Series Dinky Toy van might make a difference of 10–20 per cent over a basic one since *none* are particularly common, while for a Matchbox model this difference can be many-fold.

A rough guide to the evaluation of a typical post-war model by one of the major manufacturers is best expressed in the form of a table, taking a perfect example as 100 per cent:

Mint condition, with original box	100 per cent
Mint condition, without box or good condition, with box	40–60 per cent
Good condition, without box	25–40 per cent
Badly chipped or repainted	15–25 per cent

Structural damage or missing parts, particularly on later models, affects the value still further. This does not apply to tyres, since most types can be replaced quite easily

Care and repair

A very important factor in handling old die-cast toys is the recognition of fatigue or inter-granular corrosion, to give it a more accurate name. In its most severe form it is easily recognised, for there will be visible cracks in the metal, and the model will be mis-shapen and *extremely* brittle. At lower levels of contamination, the paint may be dull, as it has been forced to stretch as the metal expands. There may be a gap around the tinplate base-plate or, in the case of a three-part model, the chassis may be bowing away from the body. The corrosion takes about ten years to manifest itself under normal conditions, and will be more advanced if the model has been subjected to damp or extremes of temperature. The reaction cannot be reversed, but certain safeguards can be taken so that the corrosion does not become more severe. Models which may suffer from fatigue should not be subjected to changes of temperature such as occur in a sun-lit window (this can also lead to faded paint). The metal requires air to react. While it would be impractical to suggest keeping the collection in a vacuum, it is possible to 'seal' the metal by putting cyanoacrylate adhesive (Super-Glue) in the cracks. This should be done from both outside and inside if possible. Sealing the inside only *may* cause further distortion, since the outside can continue to expand. It should, therefore, not be attempted on a subject with good paint-work, which would be spoiled by the glue.

Certain ranges are more prone to fatigue than others. The majority of pre-war Dinkies are fatigued to some extent, and even those with no visible signs should be treated with care, since the mix of the alloy was very rarely perfect. Fatigue is limited but not unknown in post-war Dinky Toys. It is unknown in Matchbox, Corgi and Spot-On models, though it can be seen in some of the preceding Lesney and Mettoy die-casts. Post-war ranges in which it is relatively common include Timpo, Crescent, Benbros/Zebra and Morestone/Budgie.

To repaint or not to repaint? That is the question and there is no all-embracing answer. Largely, it is a question of individual taste, rather than of value, if you are considering the model for your own collection. In general, if the interest is in the vehicles themselves rather than in the toys as collectors' items, great savings can be made in restoring shabby or repainted examples, and it can be a satisfying activity. However, it is not a good idea from the point of view of re-sale, since there is little or no difference between the shabbiest original paint finish and even the best possible repaint. Most collectors who are not averse to repaints prefer to do it themselves, and will not pay for someone else's work.

To do a good repaint, the model should first be dis-assembled, particularly if there are plastic parts which can be ruined by paint-stripper; (which will not usually affect the metal). This is best achieved by drilling out the rivets or, in the case of a three-part model, by pinching the axle ends in a vice. If this is done carefully, the axles can be re-used. The model should be thoroughly scrubbed with a toothbrush under running water prior to painting. Aerosol car paints give good results quickly and easily, though hand-painting with modelling paints can be equally rewarding.

Bent metal should be heated, for instance with a cigarette lighter, before any attempt is made to straighten it, and it is best done in small stages. No attempt should be made to straighten metal which may be fatigued. In the event of broken parts, quick but fragile repairs can be achieved with Super-Glue but for more durable results epoxy resin adhesives should be used.

A large range of reproduction parts is now available for restoring old toys, particularly for Dinky and Matchbox models up to 1960. Most of these are cast in white metal, for example, drivers and steering-wheels for 1950's open cars, radiator grilles for pre- and early post-war vehicles and even complete baseplates for the 24 Series cars. All of these can be easily distinguished from the originals, and yet are accurate enough to make complete restorations possible. Nearly all varieties of rubber tyre used are available in reproduction, as are transfers for both pre- and post-war vans.

DINKY TOY 2-TONE SALOONS OF THE 1950'S

Top Row   156 ROVER 75 1956–58 B ● 156 ROVER 75 1956–58 B ● 157 JAGUAR XK 120 1956–58 B ● 157 JAGUAR XK 120 1956–58 B
2nd Row   161 AUSTIN SOMERSET 1956–58 B ● 161 AUSTIN SOMERSET 1956–58 B ● 154 HILLMAN MINX 1956–58 B ● 154 HILLMAN MINX 1956–58 B
3rd Row   159 MORRIS OXFORD 1956–58 B ● 159 MORRIS OXFORD 1956–58 B ● 152 AUSTIN DEVON 1956–58 B ● 152 AUSTIN DEVON 1956–58 B
4th Row   139B/171 HUDSON COMMODORE SEDAN 1950–56 B ● 171 HUDSON COMMODORE SEDAN 1956–58 B ● 171 HUDSON COMMODORE SEDAN 1956–58 B ●
            139B/171 HUDSON COMMODORE SEDAN 1950–56 B
5th Row   170 FORD FORDOR SEDAN 1956–58 B ● 170 FORD FORDOR SEDAN 1956–58 B ● 164 VAUXHALL CRESTA 1957–60 B ● 164 VAUXHALL CRESTA 1957–60 B

Making a collection

It is an unfortunate aspect of the current popularity of old toys that unless the financial resources really are limitless the choice of theme must be made at an early stage, particularly if it is felt that the interest could expand. Toys *do* become obsessive! Obviously the choice is governed by personal taste. Typically, the theme is chosen along one of three basic patterns: models by a particularly toy manufacturer (for example, Dinky Toys); models of a particular type of vehicle (fire engines, saloon cars); or models of a particular make of car (for example, Ford). Some limitation on period will be necessary. Even with the crude choice 'what I like' one or other of these patterns will become apparent whether it has been deliberately chosen or not. Not that one should be too dogmatic or limited: Dinky Toy Ford saloon cars of the 1950's would net a total collection of 2!

A good starting point is to get an idea of what is available and of typical price ranges before making any kind of choice, and in this respect today's novice collector has considerable advantages over previous generations. A great number of collectors' toy shops have been established in the last few years, and most large towns have at least one.

In addition, the number of swapmeets has risen enormously so that there is usually at least one every weekend. Swapmeets are exclusively for collectors' toys, and typically have in the region of 100 stall-holders, from full-time dealers to collectors, thinning out their duplicate models. The word 'swapmeet' has become something of a mis-nomer, as most deals involve buying and selling, though most regular stall-holders will accept other models in part exchange. A good swapmeet can provide the newcomer with an idea of what is available and of which collectors' shops may be worth visiting. Details of how to find both shops and swapmeets are given in the collectors' journals listed at the end of the book.

Swapmeets will also dispel the notion that there can be a set market price for any toy, since prices can vary enormously from stall-holder to stall-holder. However, on a 'scarcity-for-scarcity' basis, the following listing expresses a descending value in price-range-per-theme: vans with advertising; large commercials; sports cars; saloon cars; small commercials; earth-moving equipment. This pattern does not emerge in the case of Matchbox models, since these are more often collected by *series* rather than by subject.

It will also be clear that certain manufacturers are more desirable than others, and this will be reflected in the price. For example, a Dinky Toy model from the 1960's will generally be more valuable than a similar Corgi Toy model even though it may not be as well made. Even this situation is changing as the first people who had Corgi Toys in their youth (the 25 to 30 age group) can now afford to affect the market. This is an important aspect from the point of view of investment. Certain 1950's lines have reached artificially high price levels because they were being collected for investment purposes, and have consequently become bad investments. However, given that the price-range-per-theme pattern outlined above has been constant for some years and will probably continue to be so, a reasonably safe investment would be in items of similar quality in the same themes from the 1960's, this being the growth period.

Whether the models are being collected for investment or for pure nostalgia will determine to some extent the collector's tolerances with regard to condition. The investment-conscious collector is likely to choose only models in perfect condition, while the cost-conscious collector will find unboxed examples better value for money.

Storage and display

As mentioned in the section on care and repair, die-cast models should be kept in a dry atmosphere at constant temperature away from direct sunlight, and if possible should be protected from long-term exposure to dust as this can dull the paint-work. The ideal display cabinet has fairly narrow glass shelves so that each model is visible, but custom-made glass cabinets can be expensive, so for most collectors it is a matter of luck as to what is available second-hand. Original boxes can present a problem as they require more storage space than the models themselves.

The monotony of rows of similar vehicles can be relieved by the inclusion of period petrol pumps, road signs or small figures of appropriate scale.

Information and further reading

Useful Addresses

Collectors' periodicals

Collectors' Gazette, c/o Elaine Hill, 17 Adbolton
Lodge, Whimsey Park, Carlton, Nottingham.
Information on swap meets and collectors' shops.
Six issues a year.

Modellers World, 15 Bell Lane, Eton Wick, Windsor,
Berks SL4 6LQ.
Information on particular ranges and themes and
current models.
Four issues a year.

Model Auto Review, P.O. Box MT1, Leeds LS17 6TA.
Information on particular ranges and themes and
current models.
Four issues a year.

Spare part producers and stockists

Postal sales only

Dave Jones, 72 California Road, Tividale, Warley, West
Midlands, B69 1SP.
Taylor and Barretts, Britains, Johillco

Anthony Bates, 60 Fullerton Road, Byfleet, Weybridge,
Surrey.
Lesney and Dinky, transfers

Pirate Models, 430 Hoe Street, Walthamstow, London
E17 9AA.
Dinky and Tootsietoy, tyres.

Mikansue, 15 Bell Lane, Eton Wick, Windsor, Berks
SL4 6LQ.
Dinky and Tootsietoy.

Books

A History of British Dinky Toys 1934–1964, Cecil
Gibson, published by Mikansue and Modellers'
World, 1973.

Dinky Toys 1964–1980, Ed Symons, published by the
author, 1982.

Dinky Toys and Modelled Miniatures, Mike and Sue
Richardson, published by New Cavendish Books,
1981. (This also covers aeroplanes, ships, figures and
trains)

A Concise Catalogue of 1–75 Series 'Matchbox' Toys,
Geoffrey Leake, published by the author, 1981.

*Collectors' Catalogue of 'Matchbox Models of
Yesteryear'*, H. M. & T. J. Gunner, published by the
authors, 1981.

Corgi Toys, The Ones with Windows, James Wieland
and Dr Edward Force, published by Motorbooks
International, 1981.

Spot-on Die-cast Models by Tri-ang, Graham
Thompson, published by Haynes, 1983.

Valuation

The valuations given in the captions are for examples in the condition shown in the photograph. Where it can exist, the original box is assumed to be present. For a guide to assessing the value of an example in better or worse condition than is shown, please refer to the chapter on collecting.

Some of the models shown are in unusual colours or liveries, and this will be noted in the captions. Again, reference should be made to the chapter on collecting for a guide to the extent to which the value is affected.

The value ranges, *which should be taken as an approximate guide only*, are:

A less than £10
B £10 to £25
C £25 to £50
D £50 to £100
E over £100

Particularly valuable items are marked E*

Acknowledgements

The publishers would like to express their sincere gratitude to the following people for providing toys for the photographs from their stock and treasured private collections

Chris Upjohn
Bimbo Collectors Toys and Steam Models
PO Box No 6
Haslemere, Surrey, GU27 3LX

Vic Bailey
Veteran and Vintage Models
54 High Street
Portslade Old Village
Sussex, BN4 2LG

Pete McAskie and Patrick Trench
Grays Mews Antique Market
Davies Mews
London, W1

Stephen Abis

Photographs taken by Robert Cotton, Hanover Studios.